"Free me," the tribesman said. "I will walk ahead of you."

Bolan hesitated.

"I cannot outrun your bullets." The *bedu* indicated the warrior's Uzi. "I can find the best path to follow."

Bolan unlocked the handcuffs. The man stepped off the ATV, carefully scanning the ground as he plodded up the wind-cut passageway. Then he turned, waving Bolan and Danny forward.

The nomad was moving faster now, until he skipped sideways with several nimble steps.

Bolan was halfway up the slope when he saw the man's odd maneuver. The Executioner jammed on the brake.

With horror Danny suddenly realized why Bolan had been so reluctant to release the guy. Near the right front tire of the Hog, the wind had blown away enough sand to reveal a dark metal lump.

The desert thief had led them straight into a mine trap!

MACK BOLAN

The Executioner

DON PENDLETON's EXECUTIONER

MACK BOLAN

Hellfire Crusade

A GOLD EAGLE BOOK FROM

W✷RLDWIDE

TORONTO • NEW YORK • LONDON • PARIS
AMSTERDAM • STOCKHOLM • HAMBURG
ATHENS • MILAN • TOKYO • SYDNEY

First edition March 1986

ISBN 0-373-61087-4

Special thanks and acknowledgment to
Alan Bomack for his contributions to this work.

Printed in Canada

If a nation values anything more than freedom,
it will lose its freedom; and the irony of it
is that if it is comfort or money that it values
more, it will lose that too.

—Somerset Maugham

The enemies of freedom are legion; but I am not
afraid to face them, for I do not fight alone. There
are decent people everywhere who also fight the
good fight, each in his or her own way, to keep the
torch of Liberty burning bright. Comrades at arms,
I salute you!

—Mack Bolan

In memory of the thirteen dead, including four U.S. Marines and two American businessmen, who were gunned down by rebels in the San Salvador café massacre, June 1985.

1

Mack Bolan snugged the customized Heckler & Koch tighter into his shoulder. The polished stock felt cool against his cheek. He activated the Hensoldt scope in a dry run, then glanced at his watch. He had thirty seconds to use the red LED spot for sighting on his target.

He slowly tracked left, scanning the curve of the hairpin bend that was gouged in the steep flank of the hills overlooking Drakos.

Bolan selected the precise place for the hit, mentally marking it by the position of an oddly shaped yellow rock; then he lowered the rifle and began to make a fine adjustment to the butt pad.

Below his carefully chosen vantage point, Bolan observed that the lights of Drakos were already twinkling in the encroaching dusk. A convoy of trucks leaving the docks looked like miniature toys from this elevation.

The Executioner noticed that none of the traffic turned off at the intersection far below his aerie. He figured few drivers would willingly risk the mountainous shortcut after dark.

This was the quickest and quietest route across to Katreus, and it was the road Gershen would use to get there.

Satisfied with his preparations, Bolan rested his back against a boulder and worked the weapon's well-oiled mechanism. Everything was ready, and he had time.

He could wait for Gershen.

Enveloped by the growing darkness, Bolan mentally reviewed the man's activities.

Gershen's line of business was computer components, usually bought through dummy companies, but stolen if necessary. He then smuggled this high-tech hardware from the States into Canada, and from there they were sold to France under forged paperwork, then shipped on to Greece.

A Black Sea freighter carried the precious cargo on the final leg from Katreus to Odessa. Gershen had engineered this pipeline and lived a good life on the profits of his illicit trade.

His treacherous pursuits had finally attracted the attention of both the FBI and the CIA. However, the more immediate threat to his safety was posed by Thomas Loomis, a pipe-smoking investigator for Technilok Security who had cracked every case of industrial espionage he'd taken on. And Loomis was hot on Gershen's trail.

But he had not counted on another kind of heat, in the form of hurtling lead, waiting to put him out of business permanently.

Yes, Jago Gershen was very good at what he did.

Very professional.

He deserved the Executioner.

And the coldly efficient H & K PSG1.

When it came to termination, they, too, were state of the art.

JAGO GERSHEN'S FACE CREASED into a thin smile as he congratulated himself on his timing. He had chosen the right moment to get out. The U.S. federal agents were tied up in red tape in Canada. And Loomis was still methodically checking out leads in Marseilles. The secret of Gershen's success so far lay in always staying one step ahead.

He swung the Mercedes to the left up the mountain road, then noted the time on the German luxury car's dashboard clock. Fifty minutes still remained before the Russian ship was due to sail. He would make it with time to spare.

Gershen had served his Soviet masters well. There was no way they would refuse him sanctuary now, not with the papers he carried in his aluminum briefcase: the parallel processor plans for the Supercyber 3000. The blueprints for this intricate maze of module arrays would more than cover his ass.

BOLAN STOWED THE FIELD GLASSES and took up his firing position. The off-white Mercedes appeared like a pale ghostly chariot in the scope.

The Executioner heard the change in the engine's pitch as the driver shifted down coming out of the bend, then gunned the sedan up the next incline.

Bolan led by a fraction and squeezed the trigger.

The right front tire shredded.

There was no time for Gershen to regain control as the car skidded toward the unprotected shoulder. The Mercedes slithered sideways over the cliff edge. The traitor was trapped behind the wheel, screaming as the vehicle plummeted all the way down until it hit an outcrop.

The car exploded in a fireball of white-hot flame, oil-black smoke, splintered glass and myriad fragments of torn and twisted metal.

Bolan watched impassively as the burning wreckage bounced off the rock face once more and rattled across the scree below. Jago Gershen was now one more careless tourist who had become a statistical fatality.

JAMIL HUSSEIN PAUSED to light a cigarette. He fumbled the first two matches and only lit it on the third attempt. This seemingly clumsy pantomime bought time to check both sides of the boulevard behind him and across the broad square ahead.

He was being very cautious. Exactly the way he had been trained. And Hussein had proved an apt pupil in the Yemen and at Moscow.

Hussein first tasted the high-voltage charge of radical power when he whipped up the fervor of the crowds outside the U.S. embassy in Tehran. Then, together with his fellow university students, he had stormed the gates on that fateful Sunday morning in November 1979.

He would never forget the thrill of seizing control and jeering at the impotent Americans.

The streets were relatively clear at this time of night. Faint traces of steam wafted up from the air exhausts of the metro system beneath his feet. And the wet midnight pavements of Paris were smeared with the pastel reflections of the city lights.

Confident that no one was following him, Hussein strode purposefully toward the art nouveau entrance of the metro station. This was to be his biggest assignment yet, and he could not afford to get careless.

Hussein had quickly attracted the interest of Soviet recruiters when he proved to be one of the most callous of the student captors who strutted around the embassy compound.

After several months of intensive training in terrorist techniques they had unleashed him with sufficient funds to form the Brigade Jihad. He was to prove his worth when he personally transported the explosives to his Hezballah comrades, which they then used to bomb the U.S. embassy annex in East Beirut.

Now he was in Paris to round up a three-man suicide squad from among the malcontent Arabs in the Goute D'Or. These volunteers had no idea they were completely dispensable; and, anyway, the money put up by Hussein's Libyan contacts was more than they could refuse.

The American Secretary of State was due to arrive next week for top-level talks in Paris. The lithe Iranian relished the idea of striking another blow against the hated imperialist warmongers.

He walked down the entrance tunnel. The air was stale with garlic and Gauloises. A train was approaching. Hussein squeezed his way through the safety gate just in time.

There were only two other people in the carriage. Hussein remained standing close to the door and exited at the next stop.

Hussein waited till the very last moment before stepping out onto the platform. The olive-skinned assassin was taking every precaution. He turned back toward the exit and almost bumped into the one other passenger to get off from the car behind.

He was big for a Frenchman, the Iranian thought, taking in the stained raincoat and greasy beret. Must be drunk, Hussein deduced, as the odor of cheap wine wafted to his nostrils.

The tipsy traveler lurched across the deserted platform. He said something but it was too slurred for Hussein to catch his meaning. One feeble hand wavered uncertainly toward the Iranian killer.

Hussein lifted his arms to push the fellow away. He was not giving anything to an alcoholic panhandler.

But the man's right hand suddenly snaked forward with piston force. It caught Hussein completely unaware. He had no chance to ward off the lightning thrust of cold steel held in an iron grip.

Five and a half inches of Vorpal blade slid between his ribs. Hussein could only gasp as the man clasped him in a final, fatal embrace. The "drunkard" still held the skeleton handle that protruded from his target's coat, then he twisted it.

A burning sensation exploded in Hussein's throat. His heart was on fire.

Their faces were close enough to feel each other's breath. The last thing Hussein saw as a crimson supernova flared against black oblivion was the eyes of his executioner. They were icy blue.

Diamond hard.

And totally unforgiving.

LAWRENCE WETHERBY HAD SERVED in the American intelligence community on four continents, and Rio Santos was by far the best posting. Leisurely lunches in open-air cafés had something to do with it.

Wetherby appreciated fine food and the passing parade of lush South American pulchritude. He topped up the wineglasses even while he kept a surreptitious eye on the raven-haired beauty being seated in the corner of the café.

"Before we discuss the business at hand, we must toast your recent promotion," suggested Marc Goldenberg.

The new station head accepted the Israeli agent's congratulations with a gracious nod.

The two men were about to discuss the fate of the elderly gentleman who sat toying with a veal cutlet at the far end of the restaurant; and sitting there, surrounded by a fragrant backdrop of vivid tropical foliage, Gunther Boehm looked like nothing more than a kindly grandfather.

Both Wetherby and Goldenberg knew better. They had to decide what action to take should the authorities refuse the latest request for extradition.

Wetherby resisted the impulse to turn for another glance at the man who would soon be at the center of

an international controversy, whatever happened.
Goldenberg could keep his eye on Boehm and his
young bodyguard.

"It's difficult to believe that that old man was such
a monster," remarked the American, draining his
second glass of chilled white wine.

The Israeli said nothing. He had tracked down other
war criminals. None of them had horns and a tail; but
with his thin white hair growing wispy over his loose
collar and those soft pink jowls, Boehm looked the
least harmful of them all.

Goldenberg wondered how a man like that slept at
night.

As a brilliant young doctor, Boehm had practiced
surgery in Buchenwald. His specialty was pain. He had
diligently sought ways to relieve the agony of German
soldiers wounded on the Russian front. The camps
had provided him with an endless supply of guinea
pigs for his hideous experiments in stress, cold and
tolerance of the nervous system.

After the collapse of Hitler's perverted dream, the
Israeli knew, Gunther Boehm had escaped via the so-
called Vatican pipeline. His expertise had been soon
put to work by the secret police of half a dozen South
American countries. He was not at all concerned by
this new application for his extradition.

Boehm had made many powerful friends and considered himself beyond the reach of any investigators.

The waiter rolled the dessert trolley toward Boehm's
table.

Goldenberg saw the color drain from his companion's cheeks. Wetherby's hand gripped the edge of their table, the knuckles white with tension. The Israeli agent had to reach across and hold his forearm.

"I . . . I know him." Wetherby's terrified eyes indicated the tall, broad-shouldered waiter. The words were uttered in a barely audible whisper. "That's Phoenix. John Phoenix! I'll never forget him. What the hell does he think he's . . ."

"Sit down!" ordered Goldenberg. "Let's not draw any unwelcome attention."

Wetherby was right: he could never forget that man...on restless nights that chilling gaze still haunted his uneasy sleep. Mack Bolan; a.k.a. The Executioner; a.k.a. Colonel John Phoenix—and heaven only knows how many other names—had been the target of a worldwide dragnet, Operation Bad Apple. Wetherby had tried to bring him in from the cold outside Milan.

The renegade American had stolen Wetherby's Fiat and left the agent stranded, shoeless, miles from the autostrada. Wetherby had neither forgotten nor forgiven Phoenix for that. Now what the hell was he doing here in Rio Santos?

The German's bodyguard barely glanced at the waiter. He focused his attention on the covered dish instead.

"Compliments of the house," murmured the waiter as he lifted the cover.

The serving plate was bare except for a silenced Terminator—polished steel lying on silver.

The wide-eyed gunman was pawing inside his jacket but not nearly fast enough to match the Executioner, who deftly scooped up the PPS 44.

The Silvertip hollowpoint tore through the bodyguard's lapel, shattered his wrist into fragments and then tumbled around to scramble his heart and lungs into red pulp.

Boehm sat slack-jawed at this confrontation with his implacable nemesis. The silencer was only inches from his open mouth when the Executioner squeezed the trigger. The doctor's head snapped back, then he slumped forward lifeless in his seat.

Bolan vaulted the low wall and plunged into the protective greenery before the nearest diner started to scream.

"Come on!" Goldenberg almost had to drag the mesmerized Wetherby away from the grisly scene. "Let's get out of here before the militia arrive."

"I knew it," stuttered Wetherby. "I always knew it. That man's a born killer...."

2

Mack Bolan was *not* a born killer. In fact, he was far from being a soulless, cold-blooded murder machine.

First and foremost, Bolan was a soldier.

The Army had trained him. They had worked him hard, honing his natural skill as a sharpshooter and teaching him every trick in the book for deep-penetration recon survival. It was the young recruit's own determination that had given him the cutting edge.

His country had set him a task—sniper specialist—and he had taken that responsibility seriously.

Mack Bolan did his duty.

And he did it well.

He had shot the enemy neither in cold blood, nor in the heat of anger. He had killed them in the execution of his duty as a soldier. Sergeant Mack Bolan had carried out his orders with consummate skill, efficiency and dedication.

There was blood on his hands. Much of it. And Bolan did not brag about it. But then this dark-haired, serious young man was never given to boasting. He left that to others.

He was not ashamed of what he had done.

He was not proud of it, either.

It simply *was*.

And Bolan lived with it.

There was another side to his character. His closest associates saw it often enough: it was his regard for women and deep compassion for all the children. They had a nickname for Bolan back in Nam.

Sergeant Mercy they had called him.

Like his kill record, this name, too, was earned. The hard way. By living it.

To kill . . . and to care. Two sides of the same extraordinary man. Two edges of the lethal blade named Executioner. He would put his own life on the line to save a youngster just as readily as he would terminate the life of a terrorist, a mafioso, a homicidal fanatic, a war criminal or the Cong.

His targets were soldiers, too, of one stripe or another. They chose to serve in the ranks of organized crime or the international conspiracy of indiscriminate terror, which in their lust for power willingly shed the blood of innocents.

Bolan did not sit in judgment of the enemy. He was not their jury. They condemned themselves by their own actions. The Executioner simply meted out the sentence they deserved.

Mack Bolan stood up for all the countless victims who could no longer speak out for themselves.

He answered back with bullets or blades or bare hands. He did what was necessary to blow away the scum.

He did what impotent governments, armies and law-enforcement agencies could not, or would not, do themselves—the dirty work they had trained him to perform.

Bolan was a fighting machine all right.

Ruthless, but with a heart.

Calculating, but with a conscience.

Deadly, but with a soul.

He was a man living on the edge.

Living large . . . all the way.

Each moment might well be his last. But he would go down fighting for what he believed in, the values that so many others blithely advocated but did not care to defend.

There were some good people combating the same evil tide; each doing what he or she could to hold back the violent forces of darkness and barbarism.

The crippled Aaron Kurtzman was such a man.

The Bear, as he was known to his friends, rumbled around in a wheelchair these days. His spine had been shattered in the firefight to defend Stony Man Farm, but the bullet had not shut down Kurtzman's brilliant mind. The computer wizard still shouldered his share of the burden in the ongoing battle.

After Bolan himself had so forcefully severed his connection with the Phoenix project, the Bear remained a loyal contact.

The Executioner was on the outside once more, waging unrestricted war the way he did best, but despite official prohibitions, Kurtzman still worked the inside track for Bolan.

The massive accumulation of data that the Bear was privy to and the complex correlations he could coax from the incredibly powerful computers under his control often gave Bolan the vital edge in this latest round of the unceasing conflict.

Hal Brognola, liaison officer between the White House and Stony Man Farm, and once Bolan's closest ally in the Establishment, knew full well of Kurtzman's divided sympathies. But he also knew the Bear would never jeopardize national security.

As it was, Stony Man's techno-wizard was a useful conduit to the big man fighting his lonely, uncompromising war against staggering odds.

Bolan returned from Rio Santos to find a bulky package waiting for him from the Bear at a prearranged drop point. Bolan collected the other mail and messages, then hurried to the secret strongbase which he shared with his brother, Johnny.

Bolan paused only to light a cigarette before ripping open the padded envelope. It contained a floppy diskette, a videotape and a note from Kurtzman.

The accompanying message had been quickly scribbled on the back of a square of printout paper. It read:

Mack—do you believe in synchronicity? The day my SCAN program, which tracks international shipments of fissionable material, indicated that certain quantities of uranium and/or plutonium were being sidetracked to a small Middle Eastern state—check data on the diskette—I happened to catch the other item on a television newscast. See video. Could there be a connection? If so, it's scary! Call me as soon as you can. A.K.

Bolan slipped the diskette into the strongbase microcomputer unit and punched up the data that had attracted the Bear's attention. Ships' names, ports, sailing dates and known or estimated cargoes of potentially dangerous material flickered in array across the screen.

It did appear as if a freighter bound from Ostend to Karachi had detoured through the Gulf of Oman to make an unscheduled call at the port of Khurabi.

Details of the manifest were labeled as only "suspected"; still, it was enough to send a warning shiver up Bolan's spine.

The crescent of the Mideast was in constant turmoil—if the ongoing Gulf War turned nuclear it could bring down the whole deck of cards.

The big warrior operated his banks of electronic equipment—having been taught by Johnny—with the same dexterity he handled the very latest firearms. He shut down the computer and swiveled to feed the cassette into the VCR. Kurtzman had sent only the segment that was of immediate interest.

The lead-in story detailed a most unusual kidnapping, before switching to an on-the-spot report filed from Florida.

The Bear was right to call it scary.

Being away in Greece, France and South America, and concentrating completely on putting a stop to Gershen and his ilk, Bolan had missed this bizarre domestic story.

The gist of it was that a high-school student, a sixteen-year-old named Kevin Baker, was about to go on trial for breaking into the Department of Defense computer systems.

The brilliant young hacker had already made headlines two years previously when he had demonstrated how easy it was for even a schoolkid to build a workable A-bomb.

At that time Baker claimed he had only done it to point up how insecure the nuclear industry was in America. The reporter noted that Kevin's lawyers would likely be arguing a similar case in his defense now that Kevin had been caught over the computer incident.

Still, the Pentagon was insisting on a stringent prosecution in the hope that this would act as a deterrent to other hotshot hackers.

On the morning he was being transported to the hearing, however, the car had been ambushed by six masked men. Kevin Baker was snatched and the escorting officers had been killed.

A startled motorist, passing in the opposite direction, caught a glimpse of the driver in the getaway car—here the picture cut from the deserted scene of the crime to a police composite of the suspect—whom he described as appearing of medium build, with dark brown hair and a rather swarthy complexion.

The television reporter quickly discounted rumors that Soviet agents might have seized the youth, but speculated that a radical Cuban group might be trying to extort payment from Kevin's wealthy family. However, at the time of the newscast, no ransom demand had yet been received.

Whether it was mere coincidence—or the puzzling forces of synchronicity at work—Kurtzman had a shrewd hunch these two seemingly isolated incidents were in some way connected.

Bolan, too, felt they added up to trouble. Big trouble.

3

Bolan tapped out the memory code; the phone automatically dialed through to a "clean," unlisted number.

"Good to hear from you," said the Bear. "At least you got back in one piece."

"You can scratch one savage," grunted the Executioner.

"He's been scrubbed already. Lawrence Wetherby telexed a report through to Langley late last night. I 'eavesdropped' on it."

Bolan showed no interest in Wetherby's account of the Rio Santos affair. The events of the past two weeks were behind him; his concentration was focused fully on the problem at hand.

"I've just been screening the material you sent. What's the latest info you've got on this?"

Kurtzman gave him a rundown. "It's been eight days since the Baker boy was snatched and, according to the most recent reports, they still haven't heard a damn thing. No threats, no demands, no call for a ransom payoff—nothing! The kid has simply disappeared."

"No leads at all?"

"Not that I can find out from here." Kurtzmann made no complaint about his confinement to a wheelchair, but Bolan could sense his friend's frustration. "My machines are monitoring everything. The only clue the police have to work with is that description of the driver; fairly short, dark complected, possibly Hispanic. They're hitting on every informer in the Florida-Cuban underworld."

Bolan had some powerful contacts of his own in that shadowy half world of crime and politics that pervaded southern Florida. He made a mental note to see what his sometime associates could come up with, but without any kind of ransom demand this Baker thing did not look like a local job.

"From the pictures they showed, that wheelman could just as easily have been a Sicilian," tossed out Bolan.

"Yeah, there's been rumors to that effect. But what would the Mafia want with a computer prodigy, or an atom bomb?" Kurtzman was not convinced by the suggestion of a Mob operation. "No, I still think it could have been an Arab team that hijacked the kid."

"That's the most frightening possibility," conceded the Executioner. "So does that shipment of nuclear material tie in?"

"The boat docked in Karachi four days behind schedule. According to a local contact, the captain claimed he called in at Khurabi for emergency repairs. But they had plenty of time to drop off a contraband cargo."

"What do you know about Khurabi? I thought that beneath all the usual rhetoric it was basically pro-Western."

"I've assembled an electronic briefing for you. All you've got to do is hook up your terminal and I'll feed it through."

Good, as always Kurtzman was on top of the job.

Bolan reactivated his machine, tapped in the appropriate instructions and waited for the two computers to start talking to each other. It did not take long.

The Stony Man genius had drawn on a variety of data banks, videotapes and intelligence digests to compile a concise overview of the current situation.

Khurabi is one of that patchwork of sheikhdoms and emirates that dots the shores of the Persian Gulf. Centuries ago it had thrived as a port for the spice trade and the slavers; in the modern age its fortunes were due entirely to oil. Colored graphs showed Bolan how oil revenues had spiraled to astronomical figures following the OPEC price hikes.

The Zayoud family had inherited power in 1946, the country now being ruled by Sheikh Harun Zayoud. There was a recent photograph of the chieftain stripping the packing from a box of the latest video movies.

"Harun talks tough at times but he looks more favorably on the West than the Soviet Union," said Kurtzman, supplementing the visuals. He was watching the information displayed on his own terminal. "The sheikh likes new toys—an endless supply of them, in fact. And he sure can't get them from the

Russians. As you can see…cars from Germany, video equipment from Japan, games and movies from America."

"Go on."

"Okay, now watch the guy seated on his left," instructed Kurtzman as the camera zoomed in on a youthful-looking Arab. "That's Hassan, Zayoud's younger brother, and he's the real power behind the Khurabi throne. Right now he's the Minister of Foreign Affairs, but while his brother plays with all the latest novelties, Hassan is quietly consolidating his own position. He's known to be a hard-liner. He's been chummy with Khaddafi and the Ayatollah."

Bolan watched as an abbreviated dossier rolled up across the screen. "So they think he was the man behind the hijacking of that Kuwaiti airliner? He sounds ambitious."

"If fissionable material was delivered to Khurabi, you can be sure that Hassan Zayoud was the customer."

"And his friends in Iran and Libya would like to get hold of the bomb," growled Bolan.

"Or he could sell it to the highest bidder."

"No, he doesn't need the money. Zayoud can obviously finance a terrorist army out of his own pocket. He'll use it for ideological gain. Most likely he'll— Hey, stop there, freeze the image!"

"That's the most recent picture we have of Hassan. The guy standing behind him is Craig—"

"Harrison. Yeah, I know him, or know of him rather. Had a good record in Nam, then he went bad;

in fact, he's one of the baddest mercs around. Harrison will sell his services to anyone if the price is right."

"Word has it that Hassan Zayoud has been recruiting," admitted Kurtzman, "but we don't know what for."

Bolan made another note to get in touch with Jeff Clayton in Toronto; he might have heard some scuttlebutt on mercenary recruitment.

Bolan did not like the way this was coming together. Not one bit. "Can you find out who the best expert on Khurabi is in the States? I want to talk with them."

"I'm working on it already. One of these machines is scanning recent publications, another is checking through university faculties. I should have a short-list for you by tomorrow. What are you going to do?"

"Make some calls." Bolan checked the time. "And I can still make the evening flight to Florida."

"The Bakers?" Kurtzman was silent for a moment, then he said, "There's been all kinds of potential suspects mentioned—Cubans, KGB, the Mafia, maybe Muslim fanatics; everyone, that is, except the most obvious, Mr. and Mrs. Baker."

"Hey, guy, wait a sec. You think they might have snatched their own son to save him from going to trial?"

"Isn't that what you have in mind?"

"No. I don't think the Bakers would have had the police escort shot in order to protect Kevin."

"Of course, you're right."

"But I've an idea that whoever did it isn't too far away from the Bakers.... I have to go down there to find out."

"Good luck, Mack. I'll track down an expert on Khurabi for you."

Bolan signed off.

He poured out a fresh cup of black coffee and set a notepad by the phone. Then he searched for the Toronto area code.

Jeff Clayton was a friend of Phoenix Force's Gary Manning. Jeff was a tough guy with a good heart and, if he had not been retired, the kind of soldier Bolan would have recruited for his Stony Man team. It was a tip-off from Clayton that had sent Bolan and Phoenix Force deep into the Congo for an appointment on Blood River.

Clayton was playing host at his adventurers' bar, The Command Post, in downtown Toronto. He picked up the phone on the third ring.

The two men exchanged greetings but wasted little time on small talk. Bolan asked Clayton point-blank if he knew anything at all regarding Craig Harrison's appearance in Khurabi.

"Yeah, I did hear he was taking a break in the sun. Look, er, let me take this in the office. Hang on." There was a short break before Clayton picked up the other phone. His tone was now less guarded. "Dan Ruark recruited him right here in the CP. Ruark was on his way through Toronto with a shopping list; he signed up Harrison and Bull Keegan."

Ruark, Keegan, Harrison...Bolan knew what kind of scum they were: hardened mercs who fought strictly for profit. Even in the dubious trade of the professional warrior, these killers were considered outcasts.

"What was on Ruark's shopping list?"

"Oh, small arms mostly, ammunition, grenades...not enough to start a war."

"Then what are they up to?"

"From what I could gather it sounded like a training program, maybe they're whipping a personal bodyguard into shape, something like that. Ruark was pretty closemouthed about it, but I overheard odd snatches of his pitch to Keegan and Harrison. He talked about pulling guard duty...sounded like they were going to be miles from anywhere. It was easy money, I remember him telling them that; oh yeah, and there would be no booze. That's all I've got for you."

"It's enough. Thanks, Jeff. But if you do pick up on anything else, let me know."

"Sure, will do."

Bolan checked his watch. He still had plenty of time to catch a flight to Florida.

4

The young woman in the car-rental booth at Tampa airport watched the tall man in a dark suit and tropical-weight raincoat approach. Linda could usually place her customers right away, but she couldn't peg this guy with the blue eyes that seemed to bore right through her.

She felt a pleasurable thrill at being so exposed and, liking what she saw, Linda gave him her brightest smile as she handed over the keys. He had booked a V-8 with air-conditioning; it was quiet, conservative and powerful like the client himself.

It took only a few minutes before Bolan was speeding west across the causeway.

Florida seemed dusty, crowded and run-down, as if it couldn't quite keep pace with the retirement and tourist boom it had so long encouraged. It certainly was not the same place he had first rampaged through so many lifetimes ago, hot on the trail of Portocci, Lavangetta and the dreaded Talifero brothers.

But then, Bolan wasn't the same man, either.

Hell, in those days he sometimes had to hit bagmen and runners for needed funds, or steal a mobster's car to give himself wheels; and often he rearmed himself by lifting weapons from the lifeless fingers of those soldiers foolish enough to shoot it out with the Executioner.

On more than a few occasions he'd skimped on supplies to make sure he had the ammo he needed to feed Big Thunder.

Not anymore. Mack Bolan did not have to worry where the next meal was coming from, nor any other equipment he might need. The Phoenix program had given him respite from the permanent insecurity of a hunted man.

But in the end the price tag had been too high.

His new war was partly financed by a fund created by Swiss bankers at the bequest of Duchess Marijana, an expatriate aristocrat who had befriended him during his personal clash with Major General Greb Strakhov of the KGB's Thirteenth Section. The Executioner also had money in his war chest from his Mafia-hunting days.

Bolan could dip into the Swiss account from anywhere in the world to furnish himself with weapons, transport or whatever was needed to continue his ongoing war against the grip of the Black Hand and the KGB-sponsored terror mongers.

Bolan's campaigns, too, had changed over the years. Now the whole world was his battlefield and the odds against him were longer. But freed from financial constraints, Mack Bolan had redoubled his efforts.

He still thwarted the dark designs of the Mafia—he always would consider that a special crusade, for that was how it had all started—but there was an even more sinister hydra on the loose: a voracious many-tentacled monster that Bolan was sworn to oppose.

He would trade terror for terror, blood for blood, slashing ever deeper into the guts of the beast, determined to cripple this cancerous network of international outlaws, torturers and political hitmen: the kind of fanatical bullies who would kidnap a young boy who had more brains than common sense.

He turned south on 19, then hung a right on Bay Drive, cruising toward Belleair. The Bakers had a small but exclusive estate on the oceanfront opposite Sand Key. It was getting dark as he pulled up outside their gates.

It was likely the police would still be there, reassuring the parents that a ransom call would soon come, even though they were treating Kevin's disappearance as a probable homicide. Bolan had scanned the reports of the wide-scale search in the papers handed out on the plane. He checked inside his wallet; he was ready for them.

He half turned to watch a flight of pelicans swoop overhead as he crunched up the gravel path. There were no uniformed men in sight.

But Bolan was not expecting the young man who opened the door. This fresh-faced kid must have come straight from the academy; it confirmed that the inspector in charge of the Baker case was not seriously thinking that the kidnappers would make contact.

"Yes?" The young man was hesitant. His eyes darted past Bolan's shoulder, sweeping the approach to see if the visitor was alone.

"Logan." Bolan flashed an ID card, one of the many from the stock he had accumulated. "I'm from Washington."

"Yessir." The novice stood a little straighter. "Come on in. My name's Chapman. I'm pulling this watch on my own."

Bolan started to scribble a number on a small notebook. "Here, this will put you straight through to the White House—the duty officer will vouch for me—use it and forget it!"

"Why, yes sir, I'm sure they can." Chapman waived the proffered reference. He was not about to start checking out a troubleshooter from D.C., not on his first assignment. "The Bakers are out back by the pool."

"Thanks," Bolan said, nodding, giving the beginner an encouraging pat on the shoulder as he eased past. "No, that's all right, I'll show myself through. You've got an important job right here."

Bolan sincerely hoped that Chapman was not going to get into too much trouble.

The house was furnished with more money than taste. Bolan glanced into the lounge, where a cluster of tape-recording equipment was heaped around the phone in anticipation of a ransom call. There was also a red phone that was probably installed to provide a direct link with police headquarters. The wall at the far end was taken up with expensive stereo equipment and a full media center.

Wendell Baker was nursing a highball glass on his redwood recliner. His wife was unpicking some needlepoint stitches that displeased her. They both looked up expectantly as Bolan walked around the pool.

The outdoor floodlights were already switched on; they made the water look unnaturally blue and the grass unnaturally green. And Bolan noticed that June Baker was unnaturally tanned even by Florida's excessive standards. Wendell, at least ten or twelve years older than his wife, had a boardroom pallor. He rose to his feet with a slightly unsteady shuffle.

Bolan flashed his ID card again and when the Bakers seemed satisfied at its authenticity, he apologized for not being the bearer of hopeful news. He stated that there were some questions he'd like to ask them. Washington needed a more detailed profile on Kevin.

"I don't know what more we can tell you, Mr. Logan, that we haven't already told the other policemen," said the father, launching into the same abbreviated biography he had recounted to all the other investigators and the press.

In the absence of any more positive action, cooperation with the authorities was the only contribution Wendell Baker could make toward the recovery of his son.

"He's such a bright boy. Very bright." Mrs. Baker echoed the one fact that had never been in doubt.

"Anything he needed to get ahead—I bought it for him," Wendell Baker assured the visitor from Washington. "I made sure he had it."

There was something in the man's insistence on how generous he had been with his son that sounded as if he wanted to quash any suspicion that Kevin had somehow arranged his own escape in order to flee his parents. It was an option Bolan had briefly considered but discarded.

"He had a private tutor by the time he was eight. Coached him in math on the weekends. Kev took tests at a special summer school and passed straight into ninth grade by the time he was eleven. He was the first boy in his school to have his own home computer."

Baker was the kind of guy who bought stereo equipment, not for the music he could hear on it, but for the maximum array of woofers, tweeters and graphic equalizers; just as he would buy a new lens for the extra f-stop it gave him, without thinking if it would make the slightest difference to his snapshot photography. Evidently he treated Kevin as another piece of expensive equipment, to be fine-tuned for a head start down those corporate corridors of power.

"We gave him every opportunity, Mr. Logan. No one can deny that."

All except one, thought Bolan, the opportunity to simply enjoy being a kid. He tried to imagine what it had been like for Kevin at school, where he had been streamlined into a class that probably teased him constantly for being too young, too small and much too brainy.

"Oh, there is one more thing. We gave all the recent pictures of Kevin to the local police and they are making copies for circulation. But June remembered she has a fairly new photo of him in a locket. It's upstairs. I'll get it for you."

"Thank you, it would be a great help."

Wendell Baker went across to the sliding doors and vanished inside. It was still warm but quite gloomy behind the perimeter of the lights. An insect trap zapped at the unwary pests it attracted. June Baker had set her embroidery in her lap and was staring vacantly at the pool.

"You do think Chip's still alive, don't you, Mr. Logan?" she asked in a quiet voice.

"Somehow I feel that he is, Mrs. Baker," replied Bolan. "Is that what you call him—Chip?"

"Yes...sometimes. He, well, he didn't have too many friends. A couple of his classmates called him Chip. I did, too...just trying to... It's odd, isn't it, that a mother has to work at being friends with her own son."

She continued to stare down at the unruffled surface of the cobalt water, slightly embarrassed to be making this confession to a stranger.

"It takes a tragedy like this to make one reassess one's feelings," she continued. "I do love him, Mr. Logan, don't get me wrong; I love him but I don't think I've ever really liked him. Perhaps that doesn't make sense to you. But I couldn't talk with him. I didn't understand a thing he said—it was always about chemical equations or computer programs. I don't think we ever just talked about..."

June Baker dried up as her husband reappeared with the locket in his hand.

"Here, I took that picture of him about five months ago."

Bolan turned back to Mrs. Baker. "Would you mind if I kept this for a few days?"

She signaled her agreement. "Please bring it back to me."

"I hope I'll do better than that," he said, slipping the gold memento into his pocket. Bolan thanked them for their help and walked back through the house. Chapman nodded and dutifully logged Logan's time of departure.

Bolan was still thinking about Kevin as he pulled away from the curb.

He doubted that the youngster had drawn up those blueprints for a homemade bomb in order to demonstrate the nuclear industry's lack of security. More likely that was just a lawyer's argument to get him off the hook.

Bolan figured that Kevin Baker had probably done it to show his classmates he wasn't simply smarter than them but that he was light-years ahead. It was the same with the computer break-in—maybe he had done it to impress a special girl, maybe just to attract attention.

Well, the boy had drawn attention to himself all right...from the wrong kind of people. And Bolan had attracted notice by his visit to the Bakers.

Someone else was logging the comings and goings from the Belleair estate.

5

Bolan cruised at moderate speed along the edge of the golf course, keeping a careful watch in the rearview mirror. The dark blue van that had been following him turned back; an Audi took its place.

When Bolan turned right the other car did the same, carefully adjusting its speed to maintain a constant distance. A coincidence? Or were they tailing him? It was time to find out. Bolan pushed the pedal to the floor.

Bolan felt the surge of power push him back into the cushioned seat. He scanned the deserted street ahead. The road he was on ended at a junction barely four hundred yards away.

The lights turned to a green signal arrow.

The tires screeched in protest as he spun the wheel in a slithering high-speed turn.

Bolan's unexpected acceleration had caught the other driver off guard; now the Audi was racing to catch up.

It could not have been the police or the FBI. Bolan was sure of it. If Chapman had used the red phone to check him out, the cops would have scooped him up at the house. Anyway, it wasn't their kind of car.

And he doubted if it was the Mob. No, the Mafia would have gotten straight down to business, looking for a fast return on their risk, either by ransoming the boy or squeezing the information they wanted out of him.

Unlike the Bear, Bolan could think of several disturbing reasons why organized crime might want to get their hands on a nuclear device. But it was unlikely they would hang around the neighborhood to monitor the investigation.

Of course a political kidnapping was a whole different ball game. Anyone treading that dangerously close to creating an explosive international incident would be very interested in knowing exactly how the investigation was proceeding.

The Executioner was nearly three blocks in the lead. There was a small shopping plaza coming up. He jerked the wheel to the right and plunged into the quiet backwater of a light-industrial zone.

The foreign car took a tire-smoldering shortcut through the plaza car park in an effort to slice their quarry's lead time. The car swerved past a small girl bicycling across to the convenience store, clipped an abandoned shopping cart, which went spinning into a lamppost, and flew into the roadway beyond.

Red warning lights were flashing ahead. A slow-moving short-haul freight was coming through from the right. Bolan gunned the last ounce of juice from the engine.

He swung over into the left-hand lanes and raced the lumbering diesel for the right-of-way. There was no room for error—a cinder-block warehouse filled the land right to the edge of the tracks—and no leeway for a loss of nerve.

The rental car bounced over the tracks as the engineer sounded a desperate warning.

Bolan squeezed through the narrowing gap and jetted into the street like a cork shot from a bottle. A fiery trail of sparks hissed out as the heavy vehicle landed, fishtailed and straightened out on the right side of the highway.

The train blocked his view in the mirror. Bolan hit the brakes and gritted his teeth. He was doing everything in his power to lose his pursuers, but playing chicken with a freight train was cutting things too close.

He turned north, running parallel to 19, then swung across toward the long causeway.

He spotted the Audi again. It must have cut over a couple of blocks and beaten the startled engineer to the next crossing. His trackers were cruising the slow lane now, but gave away the fact that they had made him again by abruptly moving out and accelerating.

The causeway was quiet. The rush hour was long finished and the late-night crowd were not yet heading home. Bolan set a blistering pace along the narrow hump of the water-lapped roadway.

A picnic area flashed past. A night fisherman dropped his rod as he spun to see this madman roar past. Bolan reached forward and doused the lights, lifting his foot from the pedal as he coasted along the shoulder—another dark blotch of a recreation area loomed ahead.

He bumped down onto the banked sand, ran on past a concession stand and rolled to a halt behind a clump of palm trees.

Bolan tore the key from the ignition and ran for the cover of the waist-high scrub that grew in a triangular wedge at the far end of the island. The sand sucked at his shoes and the sparse twigs snatched at his clothes as the Executioner sought cover.

A truck rumbled by in the opposite direction, and a few moments later the Audi sidled to a halt at the turnout entrance. Bolan, gun in hand, crouched in the semidarkness.

The causeway lights twinkled off the windshield as the hunters' car left the road. They drew up alongside the shuttered pop stand. Bolan heard a car door click, followed by a harshly whispered exchange…but how many men were there, two or three?

One stealthy shadow padded down to the water's edge, then slowly turned toward Bolan's hiding place.

Bolan poised, knees flexed, his gun hand extended and balanced lightly by the other palm.

The bushes gave a warning crackle, marking the approach of a second man sweeping the ground to Bolan's right. He was partially obscured by the tangled scrub.

The Executioner figured the odds, decided to take out the guy on the beach first. The man was dimly silhouetted by the dull sheen of the distant city lights on the satin water. Slowly the coiled death shadow lowered the muzzle to settle on target.

The sixth sense that had saved his life so often suddenly triggered its alarm. Bolan swung about, his arm traversing right, seeking the danger above him.

"Drop your piece!"

There was a third man.

Bolan frowned. The guy must have moved swiftly along the road to position himself on the ribbon of grass behind Bolan's shoulder. He held the high ground—and a mini-Uzi.

The wicked little SMG was trained on the Executioner's chest. "Throw it down . . . now!"

Bolan shrugged and let the weapon fall. The gunner who was now on his left relaxed at seeing their opponent disarmed.

"Walk up the slope toward me. Slowly." His voice was authoritative, the accent refined.

Bolan began to climb up the short, steep incline. His progress zigzagged between the bushes. He balanced his right foot on a tussock of salt grass and tugged on a nearby branch to assist his balance.

He was bending slightly forward now, hunched to present the smallest profile. Then his right hand snaked down and plucked the second pistol from its ankle holster.

He straightened up and fired in one fluid motion. The crew boss gave one painful yelp and tumbled headfirst into the undergrowth.

Bolan swiveled left and snapped off another shot. The second target took the hit low, rocking back to collapse on the sand.

The last of the hunting crew turned and fled, racing diagonally up from the beach in a heart-pounding effort to reach the car.

Bolan fired again, the third bullet gouging a jagged chunk of palm trunk as the man twisted past it. The last shot smacked into the back of his skull, blew out his forehead and splattered a streak of mushy gore across the hood of the Audi.

Bolan ran the last few steps up the slope. He scooped up the Uzi and shoved the body with his foot. The corpse tumbled loosely down under the bushes. He moved quickly to the left to check the other goon.

The hapless gunman was twisted uncomfortably to the side, propped on one elbow, shuddering with each shallow, rasping breath. His weapon, a Walther PPK, was lying where he'd dropped it; Bolan tossed it into the bay.

He glanced over at the other man, who was sprawled facedown with his shattered head nestled in the crook of his arm. There was no need to see if he still had a pulse. The guy at his feet was not going to live too much longer, either; the soft-nosed slug had mangled his intestines.

The guy uttered a soft curse in Arabic, then he said, "Not good."

"Nope," agreed Bolan. "So why the hell did you do it?"

"Hanzal gave the orders." He jerked his head in the direction of the bushes where the first man lay. The gesture cost him an agonizing stab through the gut. His elbow gave way and he sagged back on the sand.

"Hanzal said you were not an official . . . he was sure of it. Thought you were a private investigator."

"Something like that," Bolan said. "And you thought you would scare me off?"

"Yes. And now . . ." He winced as he caught his breath. "I'm going to die."

"Yes," Bolan told him. It was not a time for lies.

It was not a time for useless hatred, either. Bolan bunched up his topcoat and tucked it behind his adversary's head.

The pale wash of a passing car's headlights swept over them. The man's forehead was beaded in sweat. Bolan recognized his face. The police composite was not exact, but close enough.

"You were the driver, weren't you?"

"I drive for Hanzal. He demanded we catch you. . . ."

"Where did you take the boy? Who do you work for?"

"My home is far away. A small country—you will not have heard of it."

"Try me."

"But this will change. Khurabi will be the center of the Crescent Revolution. Hassan Zayoud—may Allah watch over him—will give new meaning to militant Islam."

"Where have you taken Kevin?"

"He is beyond your reach."

Bolan bent lower. Looming over him in the darkness, it must have seemed that the big American was about to make a final threat to wring out the truth.

"Just as I am beyond your reach. You can't kill us all." He gasped one feeble cough and died, staring sightlessly up at the ghostly palm fronds.

"YOU WERE RIGHT," Bolan told the Bear. He was calling from the airport. "Call it a hunch or whatever."

"Let's settle for a well-informed guess," said Kurtzman. "The input I was getting made me suspect a connection. So the boy is in Khurabi?"

Bolan quickly debriefed. "I figured the Mob would simply pay off somebody on the inside; they wouldn't have to stand watch. These guys were running a big risk to stay on top of things for their boss. He's playing a dangerous game."

"Yeah, but surely your action tonight is going to warn Hassan Zayoud."

"It'll put him on notice, sure, but Zayoud won't know who is on his case." It was a plain statement of fact but it carried an undertone of menace. "There's something else I want you to check out: can you trace anything on the Crescent Revolution movement?"

"Right." The Bear made a note. "Sounds like another self-appointed savior is in the wings—just what the world needs! Did you find out what Harrison is doing in Khurabi?"

"Jeff Clayton told me he was recruited by Dan Ruark. My guess is that they're training Zayoud's men for a palace coup. Ruark has some experience at stabbing people in the back," replied Bolan. "Have you found me an expert on Khurabi?"

"There aren't too many. Bill Patterson spent quite a while out there, running a survey for Allied Oil. Trouble is, he's been promoted to senior VP and is now enjoying his yacht somewhere off Nassau."

"Who else did you come up with?"

"Professor Brunton at Westfield University. He conducted a couple of extended digs there quite recently. I called him at the university but he was just leaving for a conference in Heidelberg and he wasn't in any mood for small talk about the Middle East. He said if there was anything we wanted to know about the Khurabi project we should get in touch with his assistant, Danny Jones."

"And have you spoken to him?"

"Not yet, but I can give you his number at Westfield."

"I'll switch tickets," said Bolan. "Think I'll talk to this Danny Jones in person."

BOLAN WAS GLAD to be back in a more temperate climate after the mugginess of the Gulf Coast. He had rested up in a motel near the airport. Over a black coffee he had scanned the morning newspapers: there was nothing on the causeway killings.

The police would do their best to keep a lid on the story until they had checked out the diplomatic ramifications of the triple slaying. And if they did recognize the dead driver, they would be probing any connection to the Baker affair. Kurtzman was right, though, it would not be long before Hassan Zayoud found out what had happened to his hired guns.

The university at Westfield did its utmost to look like one of England's ancient seats of learning and, for the most part, it succeeded quite well.

The walls of McCormack Hall were covered with ivy; the new library annex was faced with gray stone to merge with the older buildings; and the tree-lined paths provided a pleasantly sheltered network of walkways across the campus.

Bolan avoided the main inquiry desk and followed the signs to the Department of Archaeology. It occupied a small wing off the back of the main arts building.

He held the door open for a vivacious redhead with an armload of audiovisual equipment. Bolan returned her smile and wondered if, after all, he might not have missed something by not going to college.

The receptionist stared up over her horn-rimmed glasses and asked, "Yes, can I help you?"

"Dr. Jones?"

"Room 17B. Down the corridor and to your left."

The walls were papered with notices for scholarship applications, student club meetings and smaller ads for a ride to the West Coast and sublet apartments. Bolan turned the corner. The door to 17B was slightly ajar. He tapped and pushed it open.

The dark wood-paneled office would have been gloomy but for a large lattice window overlooking the carefully tended lawns. A woman was standing by a tall bookcase, stretching to return a well-worn volume to the top shelf.

Bolan assumed the trim blonde was a graduate student. "Here, let me help you."

"Thanks."

"I'm looking for Dr. Danny Jones."

"What can I do for you? I'm Danica Jones."

6

"You are Professor Brunton's assistant?"

"Yes," she said, moving back to stand at the corner of her desk. She knew he was mildly surprised to find that an associate professor of archaeology was a young and attractive woman, but she said nothing.

As Bolan turned to take the seat she indicated with a brief wave, he saw a large map of the Middle East tacked on the wall by the door. "I've come to talk to you about Khurabi."

"You're a historian?"

"No. No, I'm not—my name is Bolan. Mack Bolan." He decided to be as truthful with her as he could; after all, he expected no less from her. "Carl Brunton recommended that I speak to you."

She tilted back in her padded swivel chair, appearing to weigh his introduction carefully; indeed, it seemed as if Dr. Jones was trying to recall ever meeting Mack Bolan before, perhaps in a different context.

"I'm sure you don't know me. I'm not in the academic field. Let's say that . . . well, I have connections to Washington. Can I leave it at that?"

Danica Jones pursed her lips for a moment and then shrugged in acceptance. "Sure. What do you want to know?"

"Just about everything," admitted Bolan. "I understand you spent quite a while out there."

"Work on the Haufari dig was the basis of my dissertation," she answered. She went on to explain that the Westfield expedition had excavated the ancient and long-abandoned port of Haufari, about thirty miles southeast of Khurabi.

Bolan noticed that her face became quite animated as she spoke.

Danica Jones obviously liked talking about her work. Twice she got up to point out details on the map. Bolan took the opportunity to observe her both as a knowledgeable lecturer and as a woman.

She was five-seven, maybe five-eight, weighing around one-eighteen. Her long legs, trim waist and taut stomach all accentuated the firm swell of her breasts. Neat blond hair framed an oval face, with a wide sensual mouth. Danica wore barely a trace of makeup. Bolan liked that. She didn't need it.

Her vivid green eyes seemed remote, as if beneath the cool surface there was some deeply felt, long-ago hurt. Even when her features were animated with the evident enthusiasm for her archaeological adventures, she still concealed this secret vein of sorrow. Perhaps it was guilt or doubt. No matter, Bolan thought, dismissing it.

The telephone interrupted her account of diving for the wreck of a trading vessel.

"Hello...yes, this is she...oh, hi, Patricia...no, I'm not lecturing this term, it's my research semester...well, not now, no, I have a visitor with me...yes, I'll call you later...by." She was polite to her colleague but slightly distant. "Where was I? Oh, yes...we received a lot of help from the local pearl divers. And Allied Oil were very good about lending us their facilities."

"Bill Patterson?"

"Yes. Bill. Do you know him?"

"Not really." Bolan switched topics. "How did the Zayoud family react to your expedition?"

"The sheikh was very amenable. Carl, Professor Brunton, remembered to take some of the latest software as a gift. Harun Zayoud is very easily won over! And he saw to it that Salim Zakir, the Minister of Culture, made things go smoothly for us."

She pointed to a photograph on the shelf behind her. Danica was posed next to Salim, who appeared to have more than a diplomatic interest in the American scholar.

"And what about Hassan Zayoud?"

Danica arched her eyebrows. "He's not at all like his brother. He's only interested in Khurabian history insofar as it reflects the glory of Islam. He once invited us to excavate at Hagadan, the Fortress of the Rock, to furnish him with proof of how powerful were the Tamal sheikhs. They were fundamentalist rebels who holed up at Hagadan in the fifteenth century."

Bolan could feel the tumblers clicking into place. "Tell me more about this fortress, Dr. Jones."

"I'd rather you called me Danny," she said, unrolling a large-scale map of Khurabi on the desk between them.

"Okay. Khurabi occupies less than four thousand square miles between the barren ranges of the Jebel Sutaq, here, and Jebel Akzam in the south..." she began, tracing out the facts with her fingertip.

The country was the shape of an irregular oblong, with about forty miles of coastline on the gulf, and running nearly a hundred miles deep. The interior was partially bisected by the steep rocky slopes of the Jebel Kharg. The population of little more than one hundred thousand lived in the coastal capital or in small fishing villages scattered farther to the south.

"The interior is a sun-baked wilderness, some of the harshest desert terrain in the world. Hagaden is here, in the southwest corner, quite close to the disputed border. The fortress was built around the only freshwater wells for miles."

"What's it like? Did you go there?"

"It's in the forbidden zone." Danny shook her head. "That whole quarter of the country is strictly off-limits. Of course, we could have gone out there under Hassan Zayoud's protection, but we had more than enough to do at the Haufari site. If you'll pass me that book, there's a picture of the castle at Hagadan in it."

Bolan quickly retrieved the volume. Danny found the photograph; it had been taken by a British traveler in the 1930s.

"I don't think it will have changed much," she joked. The fortress had been standing on the bare outcrop of the Hagadan Rock for many centuries. It was a formidable encampment.

"It seems to incorporate several styles," noted Bolan.

"You're right. Alexander the Great sent a garrison to Khurabi; one of his detachments is said to have laid the foundations. Randall de Lacey, an eccentric knight, brought his followers eastward instead of returning home after the Third Crusade. They built up the inner ward and towers. The Tamal sheikhs took over Hagadan and extended the walls and outer bastions. Defenders have been starved out, but the castle has never been breached by force."

Bolan didn't have that kind of time. Or manpower. If Kevin Baker was being held prisoner in the Hagadan fortress, then the Executioner would have to get in there alone, rescue him and get out again fast.

"Are there any other features of note in the interior?" asked Bolan. The map did not reveal any, but he had to cover all the possibilities. "Do you know of a modern army camp, a training base maybe, even an old cave system?"

Danny could not see where this line of questioning was leading to; she shook her head emphatically. "There's nothing else out there that I know of—just quicksand, mineral pools, unmapped wadis—as I said, this is one of the most forbidding deserts in the world."

The outline of a plan was forming in the back of Bolan's mind . . . but it would first need the trust and willing cooperation of this striking young professor.

Bolan pulled out the gold locket and handed it to her. Danny stared at the boy's picture, and Bolan thought she might be searching for a family resemblance.

"No relation," he informed her. "His name is Kevin Baker."

"Isn't he the kid who was . . ."

"I'd better tell you the whole thing . . . at least as much of it as I've managed to put together."

Danica Jones had enjoyed talking with Mack Bolan. He was intelligent and attentive. She had assumed from his guarded introduction that he was gathering information for a diplomatic briefing, or perhaps that he had some interest in Middle Eastern espionage. She was not ready for the story he now told her.

She did not interrupt or challenge Bolan's explanation of what seemed to have happened.

"Let's go for a walk," was all she said when he had finished. "I need some air."

They followed the willows down to the creek that flowed lazily along the edge of the college grounds. The harsh realities of the modern world seemed very far removed from this peaceful sanctuary. The archaeology scholar stared down at a leaf drifting past. Bolan wondered if he had misplaced his confidence.

"What makes you think it's Kevin's knowledge of nuclear devices they are after," she asked, "and not his talent for breaking into top-secret computers?"

"The bomb makes more sense in the political and military context of the struggle for the Middle East. If the Soviets are or become involved, then they well might be interested in Kevin's computer know-how.

Either way it's dangerous—for him and possibly for all of us.''

"And why should Kevin cooperate with them?" Danny tossed a twig into the water and watched it swirl away.

"They could threaten him, scare him into going along with them. Or they could intimidate Kevin with threats of what might happen to his parents. They might find some weakness to exploit, some means of bribing him. And then there's always drugs. Brainwashing.''

"Okay, I get the point. And I can see why you're concerned. There's any number of ways they could force Kevin into helping them, whether he wants to or not.''

"That's why I have to get into Khurabi quickly and pull him out," said Bolan.

"And for that you need my help?"

Bolan nodded. "I know I'm asking a lot."

"Maybe it's time I stepped back into the real world for a while." Danny linked her arm loosely through his as they strolled back toward the arts complex.

Originally she had trained as a nurse, she told him; one day she saw a news photo of a soldier carrying a child out of a burning village. They were both wounded and in need of aid and so, a few months later, Danica Jones was serving in Nam.

She sketched out her career there in a few terse phrases. Little more was needed. Bolan, too, had shared that nightmare.

Now it all made sense to him. He knew full well the pain she shielded from others who had no understanding of what had happened out there, those who could not comprehend what that meat-grinder war did to people.

For him, of course, it had never ended.... One day he had been stalking Charlie through that stinking undergrowth, the next he was tracking soldiers no less cunning and ruthless through the twisted jungle of the underworld. Sergeant Mercy became the Executioner, born of a necessity for justice, not out of a lust for killing.

Others had needed to start afresh. It was not difficult to sympathize with this woman. He could see why she had chosen to immerse herself in books, to seek refuge in a study of the past and to find solace in the peace and quiet of a small college community.

"So I guess it was at Da Nang that I first heard of you," she finished softly. "I think you must be the same Sergeant Mack Bolan."

He stopped in his tracks and turned to face her.

"Do you remember Leo Cameron?" she asked him.

"Yes." How could he forget? Three good men were lost on that mission. A small squad under the command of Captain Nile Barrabas had been sent deep into the jungle to rescue Cameron from a Vietcong stockade. They were to bring him out alive—or dead. Those were the orders. Bolan, Barrabas and the badly wounded Cameron were the only ones to get back.

"I looked after Leo. I nursed him. We became friends," explained Danny. "He never told me what he was doing or why he was so important. He didn't say much about what they did to him in prison, but you didn't need to be a medical expert to guess. But he did tell me about the guys who risked everything to pull him out. You were quite a hero! And I don't think he was exaggerating. I'm glad you told me your name.''

"So am I," admitted Bolan. Very glad.

"Then we'd better get back to my office. This is going to require some careful planning."

7

"I could only trace two references to the so-called Crescent Revolution for you," said Kurtzman, after Bolan had reported on his meeting with Danny Jones. "It's been mentioned by advisors close to Khomeini. And an inside contact reports that Hassan Zayoud referred to this coming revolution in a speech he made to a meeting of senior ministers within the Pan-Arabic League."

"Zayoud! It's all coming together."

"Yeah," said the Bear. "And I've got a feeling we're all going to hear a lot more about this unless you nip it in the bud."

Kurtzman was not a field agent—he was a genius with those computers—but Bolan could still sense his colleague's frustration at being trapped in the mobile prison of his wheelchair.

"I need some up-to-the-minute surveillance on Khurabi," requested Bolan. "Specifically, I want pictures of the fortress at Hagadan."

There was a long pause at Kurtzman's end. "That's a tall order, Mack. I'm going to have to pull strings with the National Reconnaissance Office, the NSA, the Pentagon and I don't know how many other agencies."

"If you can't twist enough arms, then use those smart machines of yours. If Kevin Baker managed to break into the Defense Department's system, then I'm sure you figured out how to penetrate the NRO network long ago."

"Okay. Don't ask me for the details," said the Bear, chuckling, "but I'll get it done somehow. Anything else?"

"Grimaldi." Bolan would have to call on the best pilot around if he was to get in and out of Khurabi in one piece. "Ask him to stand by... I'll need a long-range cargo. No official markings."

"What about equipment?"

"I'm going down to see Red Chandler."

"He's a crazy man!"

"Yeah... like a fox."

THE VEHICLE BOUNCED across an empty ditch, then the engine gave a muffled snarl as the tracks dug into the sand and propelled it up the steep slope beyond. As they slithered over the rise, Chandler shouted, "Target at two o'clock!"

Bolan scanned right, spotted the plywood cutout of a battle tank and tracked forward twenty degrees with the tube balanced on his shoulder. Chandler slowed for a second as they chewed their way across a gravel flat. Bolan, legs braced, let the cross hairs settle on target and unleashed the projectile.

The detonation shattered the desert calm as plywood splinters, cactus pulp and sagebrush erupted in a choking cloud of sand.

Chandler was off and running again.

"So what do you think of my little Tiger Cub?" he shouted. "Hey, troops at ten o'clock!"

Bolan had already spotted the cardboard cutouts half concealed in the creosote bushes. His assessment of Chandler's machine was drowned out by the staccato roar of the M-60.

Bolan pivoted the gun in its mounting as Chandler slewed the Tiger Cub broadside to the targets, before accelerating away in a spray of flying grit.

With the targets so ably disposed of, Red Chandler headed back down the range toward the main compound well pleased with the performance of his latest invention.

The Tiger Cub, as Chandler had dubbed this new creation, was a lethal hybrid between an ATV, a miniature half-track and an armored golf cart. It could carry two men and a full complement of firepower across the toughest terrain to knock out advancing tanks, scouting platoons and even aircraft.

Red Chandler, a staunch individualist, could not compete head-on with the huge military-industrial conglomerates that got the billion-dollar contracts for ever more sophisticated tanks, missiles and computerized weapons systems.

But Chandler knew that if the bombs were not used—or even after they had gone off—then the outcome of the next major conflict would likely depend on small, highly mobile units that could still hit and run with maximum force and effectiveness. He had converted an unprofitable ranch in the Southwest into a private testing ground, complete with its own airstrip and firing range, to try out his high-tech approach to the traditions of guerrilla warfare.

He wasn't getting rich, but he made a living. Delta Force had contracted Chandler to supply them with some of his unconventional weaponry. And the Rangers were interested in a lightweight, long-range glider he had developed.

Bolan had come to depend on Andrzej Konzaki, the brilliant weaponsmith for the Stony Man operation, to supply his special needs. But Konzaki had been taken out by Lee Farnsworth's bloody conspiracy to destroy the Phoenix team. Another fallen comrade...

Bolan had learned of an addition to the Phoenix program, a replacement for Konzaki called John "Cowboy" Kissinger. But the soldier was reluctant to tie up the services of the new Stony Man armorer. Perhaps on another mission.

Gary Manning had been the one to recommend Red Chandler. He had a reputation for being eccentric, but Bolan quickly appreciated Chandler's unorthodox imagination.

"You're asking for some very expensive pieces." Chandler scratched at his ginger stubble. "I mean, they're prototypes...I couldn't put a price on them."

Bolan stared at the undulating haze that smudged the horizon. What could he say? The chance that he would be able to return any of Chandler's equipment was extremely remote.

Red Chandler had laid down the rules. Despite the urgency of the situation, Bolan played the game Chandler's way. First they tried out Red's latest toy—

the Tiger Cub. Then they discussed tactics, military history, the latest developments in the weapons market... finally, Red Chandler conducted a monologue on the merits of doing business with Bolan.

"That Sand Hog you want is one of a kind. And as for the ultralight..." Chandler knew that Bolan's credit was good—for virtually any amount. And he was also certain that this taciturn warrior would not ask him for these items unless Bolan was playing for the highest stakes imaginable.

"And on top of everything else you want all this stuff crated up to look like anything but what it is!"

Chandler rubbed his hand over his close-cropped coppery hair. It was already turning grayish white over the ears—helping Mack Bolan was going to complete the process.

"I really need it, Red," said the soldier. "By tomorrow morning."

"And they call me crazy!" retorted Chandler. Then he stuck out his hand, saying, "Okay, but I want a full report on how each piece performs under battle conditions."

"It's a deal. I'll have Grimaldi fly in tomorrow."

FORTY-EIGHT HECTIC HOURS after leaving for Florida, Bolan was back at his base. Danny Jones flew in from Westfield to join him.

"Any problems getting away?" he asked her.

"No. This is my semester off. I'm supposed to be doing writing and research. What could be more natural than my going back to the Haufari dig for a short visit?"

"Did you call the Minister of Culture?"

"Salim Zakir was in a meeting with the sheikh. But I left a message with his office." Danny poured them both strong coffee.

The table was littered with notepads, equipment checklists, maps—the Executioner's order of battle. Despite the speed with which this operation was being mounted, Danny appreciated just how thoroughly Bolan prepared for action.

She could not deny a surge of excitement at briefing him on Khurabi and discussing the best approaches to Hagadan, but at the same time it was mixed with trepidation for Danny knew their safety, perhaps even their lives, depended on getting it right. They had only one shot at pulling it off. No consolation prizes.

"Look, you might think this is a dumb question, but why not hand over the whole matter to Sheikh Zayoud? I'm sure he'd take action when he knows the score."

"That was the first option I considered. There are a couple of problems, though. First, how much would it take to persuade Zayoud that his own brother is plotting against him? And, once convinced, he might unleash everything against Hassan—with Kevin still being held hostage in the cross fire. Secondly, if Hassan Zayoud got word of what was happening, it might precipitate him into staging a coup right now. Either way, things could turn into a bloodbath."

"This way at least you preserve some element of surprise."

"Yes. When Kevin is safe, we can then explain things to Harun Zayoud."

A buzzer called Bolan's attention to the computer. It was the Bear.

"What's new?"

"They're still keeping a lid on the Florida kills. From what I can monitor they still haven't figured out the connection."

"If and when they do, the whole affair will have to plod its way through the regular diplomatic channels." Bolan watched the images on the video screen.

There was no mistaking the high-altitude view of the desert fortress; the layout of Hagadan was already imprinted on Bolan's memory. The match was perfect. Succeeding photos brought the brooding structure into close-up, the foreshortened shadows indicating that the surveillance had taken place in the early afternoon. The definition was good enough to count a number of vehicles parked in the courtyards.

"Three Jeeps plus a couple of army trucks," commented Kurtzman. "And that looked like a Land Rover on the approach road. Quite a lot of activity."

"Yeah. And that could be a generator truck parked against the wall." Bolan could make out the tiny figures of sentries posted on the ramparts, but the photos were too grainy to permit positive identification of nationality or uniform.

Danny had moved across to stand behind Bolan, her hand resting lightly on his shoulder. He felt the sudden tension in her fingers as the final picture in the series flashed on the screen.

A white stallion was being paraded around the outer yard. A small group was watching the magnificent horse. The four guys standing back in a semicircle might have been the bodyguards for the man seated at the center; sitting cross-legged beside him was a slighter figure.

"Kevin?" Bolan wondered aloud.

"That's the way I read it," said Kurtzman.

"Zayoud has several sons..." Danny added cautiously.

"What would they be wearing?"

"A *thaub*." She was referring to the long white robe favored by the true Arabs.

"And a head cloth? What do they call them—a *ghutra*?" asked Bolan. "Looks like that young man is wearing jeans and a sport shirt or something just as casual."

It was the end of Kurtzman's transmission. The Bear waited on the line, knowing that Bolan was silently making a final assessment. After a few moments the man in black said simply, "We're going in."

"Right," Danny backed him up.

"Two last things I need from you," Bolan told the Bear. "All the material you've compiled, especially the satellite shots...I want them on one tape. And I want you to call Steve Hohenadel and tell him that everything's on as we arranged."

Bolan had already held a long-distance conference with Hohenadel and his partner, Chris Sorbara, in East Africa. They were the ace bush pilots who had flown Bolan and Phoenix Force on their mission to

Blood River. The Executioner knew he could trust them.

"What about Grimaldi?" asked Kurtzman.

"I'll call him myself."

It was the next thing Bolan did—and Jack Grimaldi was waiting.

"It's a go!" instructed Bolan.

8

"I'm taking her off auto," warned Grimaldi, glancing back over his shoulder to where Bolan stood hunched over near the cockpit entrance. "There could be some turbulence up ahead. Better warn Danny."

Bolan returned to the cabin. Danica Jones sat glued to the window, just as she had for the past two hours. She appeared excited, which brought out a schoolgirl excitement in her. Bolan liked her fresh-faced enthusiasm. She seemed even more vital, more alive inside, than she had in the suffocating confines of her retreat at Westfield.

There was an edge of anticipated danger, the keen thrill of being tested against long odds, as they headed into action. All three of them shared and savored the same stimulation.

"Nearly there?" asked Danny.

"Soon," Bolan told her. "But Jack says we could be in for a few bumps."

Danny did not have to be told to fasten her safety belt, then she resumed her watch through the porthole.

The vast arid block of Arabia, hostile and uninviting, stretched from the foam-flecked shoreline to the horizon. Here the earth's crust lay bare, without the slightest shade of trees or the cool refreshment of streams and lakes, but parched, crumpled and forbidding.

It was also starkly beautiful in its own primeval way.

The checkerboard politics of the Middle East had forced Grimaldi to plot a zigzag course, skipping this way and that like a drunken frog. The cover story over the airwaves was that they were a special team on their way to put out an oil blaze in Oman.

Jack Grimaldi nursed the big cargo clipper through the turbulence. He had fought alongside the Executioner in this part of the world before—in the big blitzer's recent war against the Muslim Madman. The veteran pilot wore a mirthless grin as he adjusted the trim; after all, Ayatollah Khomeini was only one of the cannibal contenders for that dubious title.

Grimaldi was a crack pilot, able to fly almost anything. His Italian good looks attracted women by the score. Bolan liked the guy. In common, they had distinguished service records and an enduring hatred for the Mafia. The Stony Man flying ace had worked backup for the universal soldier on more missions than he could remember. They were a good team.

Back home Bolan had filled him in on a need-to-know basis, but Grimaldi was already well briefed in this mission; what mattered was that Mack was trying to pull someone out of Khurabi.

They had pored over the maps together looking for a possible landing site—an improvised and most definitely unauthorized airstrip for a sudden retrieval op. But not a single square inch of Khurabi's rugged terrain looked in the least bit suitable, even for emergency use.

The pilot had suggested that the only paved road in the interior, which served the oil fields along the northwestern edge of the country, might serve their purpose. Bolan turned down the suggestion; they had to stick much closer to the opposite frontier.

Grimaldi resumed the search.

The Forbidden Zone was mined and patrolled. The sand sea around the old crusader fortress was out; it was smooth enough in places to risk a crash landing, but far too treacherous to attempt a takeoff.

The craggy heights of the Jebel Kharg were out of the question. And the tortured terrain of wadis, quicksand, mineral beds and barren rock that lay between those inland peaks and the sea was no place to land a plane, even for a pilot as experienced as Grimaldi.

The only way to fly out of Khurabi safely was from the same place they would be going in; the country's one commercial airport, twelve miles outside the capital.

"That's the way it looks to me, too," Bolan had told his buddy. "I just wanted the input of your expert advice."

Bolan's alternate plan was already in motion, but Grimaldi's role was still an integral part of the Khurabi mission.

The combat vet judged it was safe enough once more to switch back to autopilot, while he double-checked his computations to navigate their way into the gulf states' airspace.

"Should have you unloaded in less than an hour," he told Bolan, who had returned to the cockpit. He nodded to the communications equipment. "Incoming signals..."

Bolan slipped the padded earphones on his head, exchanging the constant, muffled roar of the powerful engines for the hollow static of the electronic network. It was Kurtzman, who had accessed himself through safely scrambled channels to update the Executioner.

"I got a few items for you. First, the good news: Steve Hohenadel and his partner have confirmed all arrangements. They can risk one run and one run only. Time and place as you specified."

"Uh-huh," Bolan said. "Okay, so what's the bad news?"

"Intel sources report a box of krytons has possibly reached Khurabi. Now KN22s are sometimes used in the oil exploration business, but they're also the same kind of switches needed to trigger an H-bomb. This get uglier by the moment."

"We never thought it was going to be a picnic."

"Yeah, well, some guy over at N.E.S.T. is beginning to put the same pieces of the puzzle together. And N.E.S.T. has alerted the CIA, the State Department and the team at Rand. Things are starting to move back here...."

And move they would. Bolan knew that a N.E.S.T. report would be taken seriously. The guys who made up the Nuclear Emergency Search Team didn't joke about the nightmare scenarios they had to deal with— and the powers-that-be knew it, too.

The big question was still whether Bolan could defuse the situation before it became an international flare-up and hit the world headlines in the worst possible way.

Bolan was trying to put out a fire all right; and he could not afford to make a mistake.

"Got a few more close-ups of the target zone since you took off," said the Bear. "Did a head count. I figure Ruark's got maybe forty men there, and they're training a hundred or more local troopers. Of course, I don't know how many others were still inside the castle when these snapshots were taken. Either way, Zayoud has surrounded himself with a small army."

This latest estimate gave Bolan pause for thought. In a way, the more men there were milling around the fortress made it easier for him to infiltrate unchallenged, but it made getting out again even more hazardous. The odds against were mounting.

"Thanks, Bear. We're still going in."

"Never doubted it, Mack. Good luck!"

Bolan shed the headset. He stretched as best he could in the cramped walkway behind the pilot's seat. Glancing down through the aircraft's windshield, he could see the vivid flames of the burn-offs at an oilfield some way inland. Odd patches of brilliant green surrounded the occasional well or irrigation system. Sunlight twinkled on a truck window far below.

"I'll begin the final descent in about three minutes." Grimaldi checked the transmitter. "Better confirm our arrival..."

Bolan sat next to Danny for the landing. There was nothing further for them to discuss. She had briefed him with every detail she knew about Khurabi, making him precisely aware of the difficulties and dangers he faced.

She had set things up in advance with Allied Oil, and it proved that her contacts with the giant oil corporation reached far higher than Bill Patterson. And, above all, she was a source of unfailing encouragement and approval. Bolan could not have asked for more.

The ex-nurse, every bit as much of a veteran of Nam's blood-soaked craziness as Bolan or Grimaldi, wanted to rescue Kevin Baker for the boy's own sake far more than for some abstract threat to world peace. Sergeant Mercy understood that full well.

Jack Grimaldi, with a feather-light touch at the controls, brought that big bird in as if it were a two-seater. Danny shook her head in disbelief and sheer respect as they rolled down the runway of Khurabi International.

"It sure isn't LAX," she warned her traveling companion. "Looks like a few more buildings, but no more planes than when I was last here."

Grimaldi followed the tower's instructions and taxied onto the apron at the southeast end of the terminal complex.

It was like opening an oven door. The midday sun hammered the concrete, then bounced back up to roast anything that moved. An Allied Oil truck followed the self-propelled steps to the side of the plane. The driver waved frantically as Danny emerged.

"Miss Jones! Miss Jones!"

"Abdel!" She waved back.

She introduced "Professor" Bolan, while Jack lowered the cargo ramp. It seemed as if Danny had dropped her words in all the right ears; a small crew of swampers suddenly appeared and worked quickly under Grimaldi's gruff supervision.

A Jeep, carrying three customs and immigration officials, drove across from the terminal.

The Americans' paperwork was all in order. The men stood there, watching, hands resting lightly on their shiny holsters, as Grimaldi barked out instructions for unloading the gear.

Danny and Abdel were stowing some of the smaller packages in the back of the company truck. She glanced around once or twice, wondering why there had been no official welcoming committee.

Grimaldi himself drove Chandler's Sand Hog down onto the tarmac. Bolan was busy making small talk with the inquisitive customs inspector.

"And what is in this crate here?" He tapped the box with a highly polished toe cap.

Bolan used a small crowbar to pry open the lid. "These are sensitive metal detectors. Archaeologists use them to find old coins, swords, cooking pots, that sort of thing. It save a lot of time digging."

The captain twirled the point of his well-waxed mustache. "And what is this . . . engine?"

"That's our generator," replied Bolan, quickly and convincingly. Damn, was this guy going to rummage through everything?

Most of the equipment was carefully stowed in the long trailer Red Chandler had fashioned from a converted horse box.

"Open it," ordered the captain. "Please."

He peeked inside two of the reinforced cardboard cartons. "And why so much, er, canvas . . . all this fabric?"

"Tents," Bolan lied. "Several of them. One for myself. One for Professor Jones. Another for a darkroom. It's all there on the manifest."

The officer was briefly distracted by the arrival of a fuel tanker. Jack Grimaldi went over to talk to the technicians.

The second official had been inspecting the Sand Hog, and not without an envious gleam in his eye.

"What is this for?" he shouted. The man was pointing at the mounting bracket in the back of the Hog.

"Oh, that . . . that provides a secure base for my surveying and photographic equipment."

The man nodded thoughtfully. Danny was amazed to hear Bolan's rapid explanations. She had no idea they were bringing this much equipment just for a cover story of a brief dig. Bolan had got enough gear here to unearth Troy single-handed.

This whole charade was making Bolan tense. He knew they were being watched. At first there had been nothing to warn him except that uneasy prickling he had long ago learned not to ignore.

The guy in the short-sleeved white shirt standing close to the tower's shaded windows was to be expected; any controller worth his salt would want to know more about a man who could fly like Grimaldi. It took Bolan longer to pick up on the second watcher.

One glinting flash from the binoculars marked the thin man in the leisure suit, who was lounging against a car parked beyond the chain link fence at the perimeter of the airfield.

The arrival of Delta-One-Niner must have been the most interesting thing to have happened in Khurabi all day.

The first customs officer was still fingering his mustache. "What is in this crate? Open it, please."

Bolan moved a lot more slowly this time. Inside that wooden box was the one item he could not coolly explain away—a machine gun looks just like a machine gun and nothing else.

9

Bolan reached for the crowbar again.

The nosy official suddenly stepped back smartly and snapped to attention. The other two promptly followed suit.

It was the government's welcoming committee. And not a moment too soon.

The long blue Lincoln, pennants fluttering, purred to a stop. The uniformed driver skipped back and held open the rear door.

Salim Zakir stepped out and with a delicate flick of his wrist neatly rearranged his robe. A second imperious wave was all that was needed to dismiss the customs officers. They climbed back into the Jeep and retreated to their office in the terminal at top speed.

"Danica, how good it is to see you again." The formalities of introduction were quickly dispensed with; he accepted Bolan as one of Danny's colleagues from Westfield. His attention was focused wholly on the young woman. "Many sincere apologies for not being here to greet you when the plane landed . . . but, well, pressing matters of state must take preference."

Bolan stood dutifully to one side as the minister offered more profuse apologies to his glamorous American friend. His elaborate greetings barely concealed an air of distraction.

Bolan had originally guessed the Minister of Cultural Affairs was little more than a PR function given to one of the ruler's favored relatives; now he began to wonder if he should revise his opinion.

Zakir looked strained, as if beneath all that flowery language it was taking a real effort of will to suppress his true concerns. Perhaps every minor Arab sheikh had cause to be worried.

The smaller states like Khurabi were running out of oil almost faster than the troubled network of OPEC could hold up the prices.

But whatever secret business within Harun Zayoud's court troubled him, Salim Zakir was determined to play the gracious host—at least as far as Danica Jones was concerned.

"How long will you be staying with us?"

Danny glanced across at her partner before replying, "Two or three weeks at the most."

"So short a visit!" It seemed their sudden decision to return to the Haufari dig conflicted with Zakir's busy schedule. "These are difficult times . . . but let us talk of happier things . . . there is much for you to see. The British team made many exciting finds at Salibra recently. The new items are all in the museum's storerooms. Come, let us go there now!"

Bolan noted Danny's genuine curiosity at the mention of the Salibra dig. But then she obviously remembered the real reason for her being there. She sneaked a second quick check with Bolan. They were working on a tight schedule.

Bolan nodded his encouragement. Grimaldi had the trailer already hitched to the Hog. "It's okay. I'll follow Abdel to the site. You must accept the sheikh's kind invitation. We can meet later at the International Hotel."

"Very well." She seemed a little annoyed to be handed off to Zakir.

"I should be back in town by about six," said Bolan. He opened his briefcase and extracted the wrapped package of videotape. "If you should be granted an audience with Sheikh Zayoud, you can give him this, or perhaps Mr. Zakir will be kind enough to pass on our small gift with the appropriate greetings."

The Khurabi minister gave a regal tip of his head. It sounded most irregular and typically casual of the Americans, but he indicated it would be his pleasure. It was also his pleasure to have Danica Jones to himself for the afternoon. This tall professor at least had the tact to know when he was not wanted.

The chauffeur held open the door of the Lincoln for Danny. She glanced back at Bolan, but he was already behind the wheel of Chandler's special Jeep. A few moments later he followed Abdel's truck and the fuel tanker toward the gate.

Zakir's limousine sped through the security gate and turned toward the glass-and-concrete towers of the capital city.

Bolan watched the blue import dwindling in the rearview mirror, as he drove in the opposite direction along the airport approach road.

The cargo carrier thundered overhead. The gutsy pilot knew he was breaking all international regulations to fly it out solo; but then Jack Grimaldi always reckoned they must have written the rule book for somebody else.

And he had the proven skills to back his self-confidence. Bolan wasn't sure if Grimaldi was making a midclimb correction or if he actually waggled the wings of that big bird.

The Sand Hog handled just as smoothly and powerfully as Chandler claimed it would on far rougher terrain.

Bolan drove past a row of gaudily painted juice stands, a half-constructed desalination plant, two cement works and a sprawl of shanties built from packing crates, wrecked auto bodies and chipped cinder blocks—the discards and debris of the rapidly expanding city in the hazy distance behind him.

The asphalt curved left, dropping down to run close along the water's edge. Weathered wooden *dhows* bobbed on weed-choked lines. Fishermen were hand-casting their broad nets in glittering arcs of salt spray. Ahead, Abdel hooted to drive a wandering goat off the road.

Bolan was keeping watch for any sign they were being followed by the man with the field glasses. Splitting up with Danny served several purposes, not least of which was that it forced the watcher's hand into deciding which one of them he would tag along after.

If, as Bolan suspected, the guy was keeping tabs on the foreign visitors for Hassan Zayoud, it would be easy enough for him to check on Zakir's itinerary with Danica Jones later in the day. Even that smarmy chauffeur could be on Hassan's payroll. Bolan wasn't ruling out any possibilities.

On the other hand they could be just as easily letting him out on a string. Bolan checked off the points he would have considered.

First, he was on the only major road heading south along the coast. Secondly, he was traveling in convoy with a truck carrying the Allied Oil logo on its doors.

Bolan knew he was a target that would be all too easy to find.

The housing, such as it was, thinned out as they proceeded down the coastal strip. On one side the sea rocked gently with a golden greasy swell. To his right, the desert looked as if it could have been used as a test site for a moon walk. And he knew it got even tougher inland.

Abdel leaned on his horn again. This time there was no one on the road. One arm windmilled out of the cab window to attract Bolan's attention as the Arab driver pointed ahead to their goal.

The road itself mounted a graded shelf, lifting it away from the shoreline, and a steep gravel track branched up from the right leading to the overhanging bluff where the fenced-off Allied Oil depot was situated.

Due to the uncertainty created by the shifting fortunes of the Iran-Iraq war, Allied had put any fresh exploration in this part of the world on hold. They were busy concentrating on new finds in the Beaufort Sea and off the Venezuela coast.

Danny had permission right from the top of the corporate tree to use their equipment storage facility near Haufari as a secure lockup for the valuable tools of her own trade.

As the Hog scrunched up the track, Bolan had a good view of the point of land about two miles farther on, which was the site discovered by the Westfield team. Everything fitted the mental map he had drawn from the study of aerial photos and Danny's detailed briefing.

The Allied Oil property was fenced on three sides of its square. The front was open to a sheer drop of nearly two hundred feet to the coastal road below. It looked as if the ancient cliffs would crumble away in one's hand; climbing them would be suicide.

On the plateau above, the company-leased land was surrounded by a high steel-mesh fence, secured to tall concrete poles that sported strands of electrified barbed wire. More heaps of coiled wire were packed along the inside edge to make a very uncomfortable landing for anyone lucky—or foolish—enough to clear the outer defenses.

Bolan liked the setup. Again, it was exactly as he'd pictured from the reconnaissance shots and Danny's personal photos. The few prefabricated buildings were set well back up the slope from the cliff edge in the unlikely event that there should be another sudden landslip.

A small baked-mud shack stood to the right of the main gate, from which a commotion erupted as Abdel clashed gears and topped the crest of the trail. Three children, a woman who was obviously their mother, a dozen scrawny chickens, a retired camel who was loosely tethered and a vicious-looking dog all rushed out into the track to greet their arrival.

The little girl, dressed as brightly as an Amazonian parrot, called out for her father. Abdel jumped from the cab, picked the youngster up and swung her around in a dizzying rainbow circle. The kid squealed with delight.

It was time—time Bolan did not have—for another round of greetings; the odd thing was, he was getting used to being called professor.

Abdel introduced his brother, Hamad, who was standing watch at the compound gate. He took his sentry duty seriously—there was a Winchester cradled in his left arm. Bolan noticed the rifle was clean and polished.

Hamad wore a studious expression as he examined the letter of permission typed on Allied's notepaper. Bolan doubted if he could read English, but the guardian was suitably impressed with the embossed trademark, which he evidently recognized.

The dog, of very uncertain ancestry, seemed to have formed a respectful bond with the big newcomer. He silently padded after Bolan as his master gave the American a tour of the yard. They walked to the cliff edge. Looking down from the top, it was obvious that no one would be sneaking in this way.

"That's the shed Professor Brunton used last time," said Abdel, pointing straight back up the shallow incline to a large empty unit.

"Good, it's the one I had in mind."

Bolan made his way back to the gate through the stacks of scaffolding, pump parts, crated drill bits, pipes and all the other paraphernalia of Allied Oil's exploration efforts. He drove the Hog and trailer into the compound.

Abdel had the big double doors open wide. "Very hot in there."

"Thanks for the warning. Ho, that's okay, I'll handle things myself. You better relieve Hamad. I'll catch you later."

Abdel retreated with a shrug. Crazy foreigners! It was too hot to work anyway.

Bolan was left on his own.

He backed the trailer in as close as he could to the wall. First he made sure the Hog was loaded with everything he needed for the run to Hagadan, ticking off each carefully chosen item against a mental checklist.

It was hot, heavy work even stowing the small crates and packages on the bed of the Jeep. He stripped off his bush shirt and draped it over the reinforced roll bar.

The Uzi, perhaps the most combat-tested modern weapon in the Mideast, was checked out and stashed for now under the front seat. Then Bolan tackled the big job.

It was stifling inside the prefab shed, but Bolan pulled the doors almost shut against any prying eyes or surprise visitors.

Even with Chandler's step-by-step instructions, it still took him four hours to complete the assembly task to his professional satisfaction. He paused for a moment to survey his handiwork. He reckoned Red Chandler would have been proud.

Everything was as ready as Bolan could make it. He would spend the evening in town with Danny, have one last night of comfortable rest at the International, make sure that tomorrow Danny was set up "working" at the dig to cover for him and then take off under cover of darkness....

If any vehicle could make it across the pitiless desert it would be Chandler's ugly baby. With its roll bars, shoulder harnesses, suspension that could withstand more Gs than those riding inside and its nubby tires the Sand Hog looked as if it could take on the Baja and beat the field. Bolan secured the shed doors, climbed into the special Jeep and wheeled around to the gate.

"Here." Bolan pulled some dinars out of his pocket and handed them to Abdel. "Split this with Hamad. I want you two to keep an especially tight watch on the compound."

The Arab sentry gave him a British-style salute. His brother simply patted his prized rifle.

The little girl waved as Bolan drove past their home. The dog followed after the car to the crest of the trail, then veered off to chase the camel. Bolan gave them all a final toot on the horn as he ran down the hill to join the main road back to Khurabi.

The sun was dipping low toward the jagged line of foothills that marked the Jebel Kharg; at least the air temperature was more comfortable now. Bolan had some time to concentrate on his plan for action and a host of contingencies.

He was facing more than one enemy on this mission, and he doubted that Hassan Zayoud and his handpicked troopers were likely to be the worst. There was also Ruark with forty or more veteran mercs, as tough and dangerous a bunch of bastards as he would ever have to face. And then there was the desert, those mountains and the blistering sun. But, above all, there was the clock.

Man and machine would have to race against time over some of the roughest real estate this side of hell to bring back Kevin Baker alive and so deny Hassan Zayoud the expertise he needed for the blueprints to Armageddon.

If he pulled this off, there would be a lot of explaining to do—to the college at Westfield, to the oil company and, if he was not successful, to the ruler of Khurabi.

Maybe Hal Brognola could be persuaded to pitch in with the PR work. There were bound to be a few ruffled feathers left behind on this one.

On the other hand, if he failed, well, no one but Danny and his closest associates would be any the wiser until the rebel, Hassan, launched his Crescent Revolution on the world.

But Bolan had no intention of failing.

Too much was at stake.

He checked his watch. It looked as if he was going to be late back to the hotel. He was thinking about Danny—about how quickly he'd gotten used to her smile, her vitality, her undeniable good looks—when he spotted the car coming up from the rear.

The Dodge must have been lurking behind that fisherman's shack he passed a couple of miles back. It was the only cover along this stretch of highway.

Bolan accelerated, but still not pushing the Hog to its limit. His pursuers kept coming on hard. There were two guys in the Charger, and they didn't look like rich kids out for a joyride.

The Executioner snaked through a double bend, straightening out as the wheels drummed on the concrete bridge over a sluggish inlet. He figured there was about another ten miles of desert before they reached the outskirts of the town. The guys behind didn't want him to get that far.

They were now close enough to nudge his tail—and that was the next move they made. Once, twice…they bumped hard into the rear end of the Hog.

Bolan juggled the wheel, retaining control, waiting to make his play.

A truck trundled past in the opposite direction. The way ahead was clear on both sides. Bolan snapped home the shoulder strap. He switched lanes fast and braked.

They were still right behind him.

This guy was a better wheelman than Hanzal's driver in Florida. Bolan was itching to grab the Uzi and empty a full magazine through their windshield. But that could blow the whole mission. Anyway, he was not sure they were trying to kill him.

Maybe they just wanted to shake him up a little with their crazy stunts; scare him enough to catch the next plane out. Bad move. They were making Bolan angry.

Okay, Red, time to test this Hog of yours!

Bolan suddenly shot across the shoulder, mounted the bank and plunged into the scrubland without lifting his foot from the accelerator.

And the Dodge still kept right on coming!

10

Bolan shook his head. They had tried it in Florida and now they were pushing him again. But Zayoud's men didn't faze Bolan one bit. They were in for trouble if they tried to keep up with him.

He threaded the needle between two barbed clumps of thorn bushes and bounded through an arid wash. The tires clawed hold of the loose shale on the far side as the Hog rocketed over the eroded wasteland.

The Dodge lost a couple of hubcaps and had its panels scratched chasing after the American driver. Although by now his vision was slightly blurred from the savage ride, Bolan spotted another fissure off to the left ahead. He aimed at the drop.

There was only air under his wheels as he went over the edge.

He hit that ancient silt bed below with a force that would have registered twelve to fifteen on any G-meter. But he was off and running true. The rear suspension boogies and constant velocity joints fitted by Chandler could take this slamming in stride.

The chase car struck the ground with a teeth-rattling jolt that threatened to disintegrate it. The last two hubcaps went clattering across the dirt.

Bolan's vehicle was throwing out a choking cloud of grit that left the others blind. They hit a huge pothole and tore out a couple of struts. The Charger slewed around in a crazy circle and was swallowed in the billowing dust.

The Hog hummed across the undulating sand, then slithered down the slope and onto the road again.

Bolan stopped the vehicle, then looked around. Satisfied that there was no further threat from his pursuers, he started off again. He'd have good news for Red Chandler.

DANICA JONES PACED angrily across the hotel room. Her small suite at the International, courtesy of Allied Oil, could have been a businessman's stopover anywhere in the world.

The recorded monotone of the muezzin calling the faithful to prayer echoed over the darkening city. She checked the digital clock once more.

She was mad at Mack Bolan. Not for being late—Danny wasn't that petty. But for palming her off on Salim Zakir so readily. If he wanted her to act as a decoy to keep the Khurabian authorities distracted, he might at least have let her in on his plan.

And she knew Bolan wanted to leave her behind to make a show of working on the Haufari dig for a couple of days. She had agreed to do that in advance, but now that she was out here Danny wanted to stick with him. Crazy! She knew the danger they faced if anything went wrong. But she felt this pull, this need, to confront the challenge that lay ahead.

It was her own confused feelings that caused this sudden frustration, Danny admitted to herself. She wasn't really mad at him. If something did go wrong on this rescue mission, then she wanted to be at Bolan's side.

The plain truth was that this man had kindled emotions in her she had long thought so utterly repressed that she would never feel them again.

This was ridiculous. She was acting like a schoolgirl. But that didn't stop her from rehearsing in front of the bathroom mirror. Danny tried on her sternest frown. . . .

Three sharp raps on the door.

Danny ran over, opened it and said, "Hi, I was worried about . . ."

She did not finish.

It wasn't Bolan.

Two men stood in the corridor; the shorter one held a pistol. It was pointed at her stomach.

She tried to slam the door in their faces. The bigger of these two local thugs jammed it with his foot, then reached forward and grabbed Danny's shoulder.

She felt that big hairy paw clamp hold with a viselike grip. Danny was lifted bodily through the doorway.

"You will come with us! Now!"

"Okay, King Kong, but you can let go of me." She tried to shake him loose. Nothing doing. His fingers dug deeper into her flesh as he propelled her toward the service elevator.

The other guy helped steer by jabbing her in the ribs with his gun.

There was a sickening chill in the pit of her stomach. Yes, thought Danny, this would have been a very good moment to have Mack at her side.

THE HOG DREW SOME CURIOUS STARES from the young dudes out cruising along the waterfront; even with the unlimited funds at their disposal they hadn't seen anything quite like that on four wheels before.

There was an insane sense of urgency about the construction of the new city. It was as if they were racing to build a modern metropolis, an unfinished version of Manhattan dotted with minarets right out of *Arabian Nights*, before the oil patch was bled dry; though what they would do with it after that was anyone's guess.

The past and the future seemed to be fighting for control of Khurabi. The spiked towers of the minarets were squeezed between the dazzling new office blocks and hotels.

Bolan slowed down as he entered the city core. He noted there were a lot of police patrols on the streets. Keeping a watchful eye on all the traffic signals, Bolan cruised into town, reviewing his battle plans once more. Maybe he should go tonight. The Hog was packed and ready for action. He'd just proved it. And those two guys in the wrecked Charger would not be stranded back there for long.

He was confident that he could trust Danny to do her part; so far she had proved to be efficient, thorough and fast. He could not have mounted this Khurabian mission half as quickly without her invaluable aid.

Bolan stopped for a red light. He was mentally juggling his own schedule with the carefully timed arrangements that he had already set up with Jack Grimaldi and Steve Hohenadel.

There were no safe lines he could trust in Khurabi, no way to set up a conference call on this thing. He was out on the end of a string. Anyway, if he started off tonight, it might give him more time to recon the fortress at Hagadan. And that wasn't a bad idea, not with the figures Kurtzman had passed on just before they landed.

His mind made up on advancing the timetable, Bolan now decided to park the Hog around the back of the hotel. He would discuss this change of plan with Danny, shower, grab a catnap and leave unnoticed. He'd be deep in the desert before any more of Hassan Zayoud's spies figured out he was missing.

Bolan drove past the floodlit display of fountains in front of the International and turned into the narrow lane leading to the rear. He glanced left and spotted a likely looking place around a shadowy corner beyond the garbage dumpsters.

Damn, another car was already parked back there. Then he noticed that the driver was looking anxiously at the building, checking his watch, nervously signaling to the people coming out from . . .

Two Arab hoods were holding Danny captive!

Bolan raced forward, working the wheel, accelerator and brake pedal down to force a last-minute skid. The Hog slammed sideways into the thugs' car. The broken body of the driver was flung back inside across the seat, his head lolling at an unnatural angle.

Using the roll bar for a handhold, the Executioner vaulted from the Hog. He came hurtling out in a drop kick aimed straight at the face of the small gunman. The pistol slithered across the concrete paving as the guy went down with his nose smeared into bleeding pulp.

Danny had shoved her full body weight into the goon who was holding her, catching him off balance. He staggered back against the wall.

The gorilla grunted with pain as the blonde brought up her knee like a sledgehammer between his legs.

Bolan had scooped up the gun and now chopped the big guy viciously behind the ear. Steel split flesh to the bone. His knees buckled and the strong-arm specialist subsided in an untidy heap.

"Watch out!" Danny shouted.

The other hood spit out a bloody curse through broken teeth. Bolan clipped him hard with the gun butt. He fell back on top of his partner.

Danny leaped into the Hog and scrambled into the passenger seat. Bolan was right behind her. The door fell off the getaway car as the Hog pulled away, exposing the dangling feet of the crushed driver. The other two were still huddled in an unconscious tangle as Bolan exited at the far end of the alley and slipped into the evening traffic.

"Are you all right?" Bolan's first concern was for her well-being.

"Yes, I think so . . . just a little shaken up, I guess," gasped Danny. "Thank you. Thank goodness you arrived in time."

"Almost didn't. Two guys followed me, too."

"What happened?"

"We had a game of off-road tag." Bolan grinned and patted the dash above the complex instrument panel. "The Hog won." Then his face became serious. "What happened back there?"

"I was in my room waiting for you to show. Knock on the door...and those two baboons were there with an invitation I couldn't refuse. They shoved me into the elevator and, well, everything was so fast when you got there..."

"You handled yourself pretty well."

"Yes, but suppose you hadn't shown up in time? I hate to think what they would have done to me."

Bolan was forced to slow down as another police car drove past. They were still in the westernized downtown area—two foreign visitors who could have been going anywhere.

Actually Bolan was taking a deliberately convoluted route out to the main road that ringed the city limits. He was constantly alert for the sign of anyone who might be following them, revising his strategy yet again and still holding a conversation with Danny.

"I don't believe they were going to kill you, if that's what you're thinking," Bolan reassured her. "We've both had teams set on us with orders to shake us up, scare us into leaving."

"There would be no reason for Hassan to suspect we were anything other than what we claimed to be— an archaeological team."

"That's why I say these guys were just trying to frighten us off. Only now, when they report in—and it's probably all radioed back to Hassan—they're going to guess we might be here for a different purpose than to root around Haufari.''

"Does this mean . . . are you going to call it off?"

"Nope. But I am changing the plan. We're going in tonight. Right now.''

Danny glanced across at him. "Did you say 'we'?''

"Yeah," Bolan replied. "There's no choice. I can't leave you on your own down the coast. Even with Abdel and his brother around, it's still too much of a risk. I have no option but to take you with me.''

11

Danny awoke to find the very worst of the day's heat was over. The sun had dipped low enough to send a blinding shaft spearing down beneath the overhanging ledge that protected them. She lay there for a moment, her head resting on a folded blanket, staring up at the weathered pink rock above her.

She could still feel the effects of last night's drive in every bone of her body. Danny felt like one great big bruise. It had been a long pummeling ride across the moonlit desert.

They had reached the outskirts of town without further incident. Then Bolan had driven south, looping toward the junction with the coastal route to Haufari, but on a deserted stretch of the highway he abruptly plunged off into the scrub and circled wide around the back of the airfield. Using the shielded headlights only when absolutely necessary, he had tried to steer a course that would eventually intersect with the line of march he'd originally intended to take.

The going had been relatively easy at first. They had kept up a good speed across the hard-baked mud flats—which were only softened once a year by spring rains, if they fell at all—but this featureless plain gave way all too soon to the rising slope of a bleached flintstone desert dotted here and there with low patches of coarse, brittle weeds.

Irregular bumps had gradually become treacherous ridges, which Bolan navigated in the darkness with some uncanny skill that had left Danny baffled.

They hadn't talked much. She knew he had been concentrating on putting as much distance as possible between them and the city by dawn.

Twice they had ended in impassable gullies; patiently Bolan backtracked and tried another route. The almost-full moon cast a cold glow over this weird lunar landscape. And the ride got still rougher.

Bolan had woven cautiously between tortured spurs of rock as sunrise streaked the sky. The awesome beauty of it took Danny's breath away: at first it was merely a lilac blush, then smudges of rose and amethyst lit up, until finally a far-off bank of clouds was transformed into flaring banners of gold.

They had stopped more frequently then. Bolan double-checked the maps, until he found this dead-end fissure with its overhanging lip to shield them from watching eyes and the full glare of the daytime sun.

The Hog was covered with camouflage netting.

Bolan was already up and about and seemed well rested. He had the maps spread out on a flat rock in front of him. He glanced back at her the moment she stirred.

"Stiff?"

She nodded, but even that small gesture hurt.

"Here." He poured out a careful measure of water for her. "That's your ration for this stop. I was only carrying enough for myself on the way in—and I even cut back on that to make room for an extra can of gas.''

Gratefully Danny took a small sip, swilled it around slowly and then swallowed it.

"Where are we?" she asked, carefully balancing the rest of her water while crouching down to look at the map.

"I figure we've reached this spot here." He tapped a point about thirty miles or almost a third the length of the country, inland from the shore of the gulf.

"Is that all we've covered? I feel as if we drove about two hundred miles!"

"It was sixty-eight miles to be precise, following along this diagonal from the city. Those last three hours were slow going and we took more than one blind turn." Bolan waved his hand to the west of their present position. "We're still five or six miles off the track I had intended to take up from Haufari."

Danny glanced at the map. "That would take us dangerously close to the frontier. There are bound to be mine fields along there."

"Yeah, but not much other traffic, though."

"Maybe some patrols, even that far out."

"You're right. That's why we're going to lay low for a while yet. But we've got to risk moving while there's still some daylight left. I want to reach the Jebel Kharg before it's too dark to scout a way across."

Danny draped the blanket to provide a patch of shade and settled down to wait. She just lay there. Bolan sat propped against a rock. Both of them were conserving their energy for the arduous trek ahead.

"You know, in all that excitement, there was something I didn't tell you about."

"What's that?"

"About my day with Salim Zakir. I've never seen him like that before."

"How was he?"

"Nervous. Real edgy. Something was going on, I'm sure of it." Danny wanted to be more specific but could not quite put her finger on what it was that made her feel so suspicious. "Four times at the museum he was called away to the phone . . . not the one in the office; he took all the calls on his car phone."

Bolan sensed it, too. Maybe it was all those cops on the street that bothered him.

Khurabi was a powder keg ready to blow.

"I think Hassan is getting ready to strike against his brother," he said, "and anyone in a position of power is going to have to choose sides."

"Then Salim will back Harun. You can bet on that. His youngest sister is one of Sheikh Zayoud's wives, a favorite of the king. Those two are very close. Salim was off to see him again when he dropped me at the hotel. Oh yeah, I almost forgot, I gave him that tape."

"Well, if Harun doesn't know what his brother is up to by now, he soon will . . . ."

Bolan motioned for her to be absolutely still. Danny had no idea what had suddenly alerted him, but something out there in the wasteland had triggered an inner alarm.

The warrior quietly levered himself up between the boulders on the far side of the shallow cut. He signaled for Danny to follow him, reaching back to give her a hand up.

"See them?"

"Where?" Danny saw nothing but mile upon mile of sand and rock.

"Way over there—they're heading south."

Now she could pick out the small dark blobs, seeming to be swimming slowly through the shimmering haze that hovered above the desert floor. How on earth did he know they were out there? "Who are they . . . a border patrol?"

"I don't think so. Looks like four, maybe five men with camels; a small caravan of some sort."

Danny shaded her eyes and studied the moving figures. "Bedu. A tiny group of nomads still sticking to the traditional ways."

Bolan nodded. In a way he admired them. Wandering warriors who had made no compromise. He could understand that, although to most people, even to other more "progressive" Arabs, it was madness. To Bolan it was a madness worthy of respect. "They must know of ancient paths across the mountains. They're too far west to have skirted the Jebel Kharg."

"I thought this was on the edge of the Forbidden Zone."

"I guess those guys don't read signs or maps. They don't need to, they know where they are. Probably heading down to the fishing villages on the coast to do a little trading," said Bolan. He checked his watch and studied the position of the sun for a moment. "Let's get going. If we stick to that old wadi down there, we can go for a couple of miles before we have to break cover."

"Won't they see us?"

"Yes," admitted Bolan. "But if I sensed their presence, then I expect they already know we're here, too."

Danny knew he was right; no one knows the desert better than the nomads.

They repacked the Hog and moved cautiously down the wadi, its sides long since worn down to little more than weak crumbling shoulders. There had been no flash floods here for many seasons.

Bolan drove with care, slowing down on the softer patches so as not to churn up a telltale plume of dust. The foothills of the jebel rose sharply in front of them, and the jagged wall of the main escarpment lay just beyond, its granite cliffs streaked with broad black bands of igneous rock.

Several times Danny checked over her shoulder, searching for any sign of the desert tribesmen. They had vanished into the desolate landscape back there as silently as they had appeared.

Sometimes glancing at the map folded in a transparent case on Danny's knee, but more often relying on the aerial surveys he had committed to memory and an intuitive feel for the lay of the land, Bolan navigated the sturdy Hog up the unseen trail toward the brooding heights.

Danny wanted to find out more about this man who exerted such a powerful attraction for her. It wasn't that she needed to rehash stale memories of Nam or even to learn his side of the story she'd first heard from Leo Cameron. If you hadn't been there, then there was no point in talking about it; if you had survived that hell, there was little to say, either. You couldn't add glory to it. You couldn't take away the pain.

They had both been there—in it up to their necks. And that was that.

No, she was more interested in what had happened to him after it was all over—although, as was becoming apparent, it was not all over for him. And likely never would be.

But this was not the time or place for personal poking about into the past. They would be lucky simply to survive the present. And wasn't that the way it had been back in Nam? Besides, Mack would tell her what he wanted her to know, when he wanted her to know it.... She sensed they had much to share together.

"Which way now?" Bolan posed the problem aloud. A wedge of reddish rock split the way ahead into a fork.

"Whichever we pick, you'd better get us under cover fast," replied Danny. "There's a—"

"A spotter plane back there," Bolan calmly finished her observation. "I've had my eye on it for ten minutes. Right now I think they're more interested in those camel riders."

Bolan steered the Jeep to the left, drove for about four hundred yards and stopped in the lee of a huge sandstone block. Within moments they had the vehicle draped with the camouflage mesh, which would give nothing away to a plane flying over.

From this elevation they could look down on the vast plain of the Khurabian desert. A couple of swirling yellow columns—dust devils, several hundred feet high—were moving majestically before the wind, drifting toward the distant coast.

"They'll obliterate any tracks we might have left out there," he commented. "Might even force that plane to return to base."

It was little more than a faintly buzzing speck, dipping and twisting above the plain, like a drowsy summer insect. He checked it through the glasses. "Must be one of the three spotter planes operated by the KDP, the Khurabian Desert Police. Zayoud's only got a handful of jets in his so-called air force. And his personal Boeing, of course."

"How do you know all this?"

"A friend gave me a rundown on all the forces and hardware at the sheikh's disposal before we left."

"But you talked about choosing sides when the showdown came...so which side are the KDP on right now? Are they staying loyal to Harun, or are they throwing their lot in with Hassan?"

"Good question. We must assume they've gone over to Hassan. I'm not going to wave them down to find out."

Danny still glanced nervously back at the observation craft, trying to keep track of it as it dwindled into the distance, while Bolan fixed his attention on the barrier that loomed in front of them.

This giant uplift, the tilted shelf of the Jebel Kharg, almost cut the tiny oil kingdom in two. Aeons ago it had been a solid, continuous obstruction, but over thousands of years it had been scoured by the abrasive sand, split and blistered by the pitiless sun, buffeted by storms, creased by the wind and washed away in places by the infrequent rains.

Bolan scanned the high ground. Somewhere between those contorted ridges was a track through to the sand sea and the Fortress of the Rock.

But would the traditional paths, those centuries-old routes of the slaver caravans, still be safe? Would any of them still be open?

Hassan Zayoud had used his viceregal powers to declare this whole corner of the country, from the jebel to the disputed fringes of Khurabi, a militarized zone, off-limits to everyone except duly authorized personnel. The tracks across it were probably blocked with barbed wire, mined or obliterated entirely by detonated landslides . . . and yet the bedu still knew of a secret way through these hills.

He spotted a movement across the backdrop of the topmost cliff. Had Hassan posted lookouts up there? Bolan swept the peaks with the binoculars.

"What is it?" asked Danny.

"Birds. Small vultures of some kind," Bolan told her. They had seen few signs of life on the trek in: some tracks, droppings, but not the desert creatures that had made them.

Dusty shrubbery and yellowed grass grew in isolated patches along the face of the jebel, sure signs of deep wellsprings and stagnant puddles among the rocks, and where there was water there was life.

"Not much out here," said Danny. "Jerboas, sand hares, the odd snake . . . maybe a fox or some oryx on the top slopes."

"That's all they need," said Bolan, still watching the patient raptors circling on the updrafts. "Over there, see that swayback ridge? Looks like there might be a trail that doglegs up behind it."

He handed the binoculars over to Danny. "Yes, that looks like our best bet. What's the plan?"

There was still an hour of daylight left. "Let's drive up there. Must be about three miles. If things look clear, we'll try to slip over the top at dawn."

It was better than four miles of hard punishment before they reached the hollowed slopes behind the ridge. In the debris-strewn gully they were well covered from any watchful eyes on the plains far below; in fact, they could only be spotted by someone on the cliffs directly above their position.

The final elevation still appeared daunting. In places the rock face was formidably sheer, but here and there it was scarred deeply by falls and erosion. One of those clefts held the key to the Jebel Kharg.

"This is a good spot to make camp. I think we can risk a small fire. It'll be another cold night, particularly at this elevation."

Bolan parked the Hog but did not cover it this time. Danny set up their camp between the Jeep and the cliff, then cast around for some smaller slabs of rock to build a sheltered fireplace. He removed what dead bushes he could find between the cracks and crevices, hacking off the tougher ones with his Teflon-coated blade. He slid the knife back into its ankle sheath, gathered the bundle of precious kindling together and brought it back to the dell.

"There is a way through up there somewhere," announced Danny positively. "I went out to gather some fuel myself—look what I found!"

"Camel dung."

"Very old, very dry, but somebody else had passed this way, too."

"Okay, you get the fire going. The supplies are in that box there. It ain't exactly *cordon bleu*," said Bolan, his hopes recharged by Danny's sharp-eyed discovery. "I'm going to scout that trail up there."

With the Uzi slung on a shoulder strap, Bolan followed the twisting path that threaded through the tall boulders above their campsite. A withered thistle, which had bloomed briefly after a shower some seasons past, still held an errant strand of camel hair. He searched the mottled mauve-and-brown rocks for signs of the trail the drovers must have taken. None of the clefts looked very promising.

A fan of loose shale, too treacherous even for the Hog, marked the one rift the traders might have come through. Bolan worked his way farther to the right, but found nothing passable. And it was getting darker by the moment.

He began circling back toward the camp. The velvet night sky was spangled with myriad stars. After the broiling heat of midday, it was amazing how cool it became once the sun had vanished.

What if he had to go the rest of the way on foot? Bolan began to recalculate his timetable with half a mind, while the rest of him concentrated on keeping his footing among the tumbled rocks.

He got a tingling jolt from his internal warning system just as he approached the camp. He thought he saw two darkly bundled figures scrambling over the ridge above the Jeep. He unslung the Uzi in a flash.

But it was too late.

A white-robed man with an evil gold-capped smile was already squatting by the fire. An ancient Lee Enfield was resting across his lap, his finger curled about the trigger. And the muzzle was only inches from Danny's heart.

12

In that small circle of flickering firelight the old man's leathery face looked even more like the mask of some evil *djinn*. With the hand that cradled the rifle he signaled for Bolan to come closer.

"No, *sah'b*...no touch gun! No need for gun." He made a small patting motion in the air to indicate that the big foreigner should lay down his weapon.

With Danny's life in the balance as a bargaining chip, Bolan had no choice but to comply.

The other two men—both younger, probably the rifleman's sons—jumped down onto the track. They both wore *khunjars*, the curved and bejeweled daggers given to every male when he reached manhood. One had a cast to his eye that gave him a menacing, retarded look.

"Closer, *sah'b*!"

Bolan stepped forward, trying to figure the odds. He could see the man was not quite as old as he'd first thought. These bedu wanderers were traditionalists— if put to the test, where did their loyalties lie? He had to guess they would probably pick Hassan's fundamental fanaticism.

Were they just being cautious about stumbling onto strangers in the middle of nowhere? Or did they intend to kill them both right here and now? The rifle had not budged an inch. There was less than a hairbreadth between those two possibilities, and Bolan was not going to bet on the difference. Not yet.

He spread open his empty hands, palms showing, "Whatever we have is yours—please, share our meal."

The leader appreciated the courtesy, even though both he and Bolan knew the old-timer was in a position to take what he wanted. Yet he was still more curious about their mysterious presence here than eager for the coffee, which was boiling by the fire.

Danny glanced across at Bolan as he squatted on his haunches. Then she quickly looked away, ashamed and angry at herself for having been taken by surprise.

"What you do here, *sah'b*? Long way from city."

"Oil. We're looking for oil," Bolan lied easily. "Geologists. We're a search team for Allied Oil."

"Ah, you think you find oil up here?"

"No, not around here, old friend. We want to prospect on the far side of the jebel." Bolan's casual wave at the cliffs above them made one of the other men bring a British army service revolver to bear. They were very jumpy.

The man by the fire translated Bolan's explanation for his companions. None of them looked too convinced, and Bolan observed the puzzled looks on their faces, as they wondered, perhaps, why these Americans would be out here in the deep desert.

"Tell you what," suggested Bolan, appearing as affable as could be, "I could hire you guys as our local guides. The company gives me funds for that. I'm willing to pay you well if you'll show us a safe way across the top of the jebel. Will you do it? Here, let's have some coffee and discuss a fee.''

The old man smiled greedily, his gold fillings glinting in the light of the campfire at this mention of money.

"There are ways through the hills," he conceded. "But this territory is forbidden, *sah'b*. Very dangerous to be here."

"Well, yeah, but the oil down there doesn't know that…and we have to go where the oil is," said Bolan, still playing the part of a modern-day prospector. "Anyway, you're out here, too, aren't you?"

"My people have always been in these parts, long before soldiers come with their spiked wire and bombs in the ground. This is our land, *sah'b*."

"Then I insist on paying you to guide us." Bolan moved slowly—he did not want anyone to get the wrong idea—as he pulled a pouch from around his neck. He poured out the contents in his cupped hand. "See, gold coins… Now, let's have some of that coffee while we talk business, eh?"

Danny followed Bolan's signal and moved closer to the crackling fire. The older man stayed squatting where he was, the rifle still balanced across his knees, though no longer aimed directly at Danny's breast, as he rattled off the proposition to his sons.

One of them replied in the high-pitched guttural dialect of these nomads.

Bolan wondered if they were already haggling over a suitable price to charge for their services, as his hand dropped slowly toward his ankle. His own smile was fixed, his eyes steady on the leader; but through peripheral vision he concentrated on Danny. It was up to her to make the next move.

Danny lifted the coffeepot away from the flames.

The man by the fire rebuked the guy with the lazy eye, obviously imposing his will, then suddenly nodded....

''Now!'' shouted Danny, hurling the scalding contents of the pot straight into the leader's face. He tumbled backward with a scream and a spluttering curse.

Bolan pulled the knife from its hiding place and, throwing it underarm, struck the other gunman square in the throat. The revolver dropped from his grasp as he made a futile attempt to pluck out the sticky blade from under his chin. With one last soft gurgle he collapsed sideways on the rocks.

The third tribesman was pulling the dagger from his belt when Bolan hit him low with the full force of a shoulder charge. They slammed into the dirt, struggling like wild beasts for the advantage.

Scooping up some dust, the nomad threw it at his attacker, but Bolan was no longer there to be blinded by that old trick. He'd slipped the man's hold, twisted around and was looping a forearm under the Arab's beard.

He grabbed hair and head cloth all in one, jerking violently and hard. The man's neck was broken in an instant. He flopped on his back with one final spasmodic twitch, his hand splayed open, and the last grains of sand trickled out between his lifeless fingers.

When Bolan spun around to face the fire, Danny had already disarmed the startled headman and now had him well covered with his own rifle.

"He told them we were to be killed," she explained. "They were going to steal our money and then take our bodies to Hassan Zayoud for a reward."

The bedu held his head in his hands, sobbing from the pain of being burned as well as the remorse for causing the deaths of his sons.

"Those two weren't so keen on the idea at first—just in case we really were working for the oil company—but he ordered them to get on with it. He promised that one your gun...that's when I yelled."

"Thanks. I didn't know what the hell they were talking about."

Bolan retrieved his Uzi, but Danny did not let the rifle waver even for a fraction. He patted her on the shoulder and she relaxed a little. Then he shook his head as he looked at the bedu bandit. The man was not in too bad shape; what a pity it had come to this. Bolan held nothing against these men. His only concern was to rescue Kevin from Zayoud's castle.

"You have killed my sons."

"Uh-huh, you called the play, old man, not me. You lost the gold. You lost your boys. And if you don't lead us safely over that mountain at dawn, then I'm going to track down the rest of your family and wipe them out, too!"

Bolan had no idea how he could have executed this snarled threat even if he had meant it, but the menacing warning deflated the chieftain once and for all.

He had just seen this deadly warrior in action and it never occurred to him that the words might be only an angry bluff.

He did not offer the slightest resistance when Bolan shackled him to the Hog. The big foreigner frisked him for other weapons—he had none concealed on him—and then quite calmly, almost as if nothing had happened, this strange invader poured out the last of the coffee from the pot.

They took turns standing watch. When Danny woke up to take the second shift, the bodies of the two would-be assassins had disappeared. She didn't ask Bolan what he had done with them.

They switched lookout shifts once more during the night.

Bolan did not appear to stir as he rested, but Danny had little doubt his automatic warning system remained on full alert even while he slept. She padded over to check on their native prisoner, who somehow managed to doze fitfully with one arm held uncomfortably upright. He was secured by the wrist to the roll bar.

She was well aware by now that Mack seemed to have covered every angle—but why had he brought along those steel handcuffs?

Danny turned to look at him but Bolan was no longer there.

She saw him sauntering back from behind the rocks as the sun, still unseen, splashed the first vivid rays across the dawn sky.

He packed up the last of their things, then stood over the chief. "Remember what I told you?"

The bedu did, only too well. "I will show you the way."

"No tricks."

"Oh no, *sah'b*—upon my honor!"

"Then let's go."

Danny rode in back with the gear. The Hog scrambled along the slope, all four wheels driving it hard up the dangerous incline.

The Arab pointed ahead to what appeared to be a dead end, so well did the colors of the rock blend into a seamless whole. Bolan approached with caution.

The trail hooked sharply, disappearing through the granite shoulders of a gap barely wide enough to admit the armored Jeep. Beyond this concealed entrance it widened out and, except for one large flattened rock that partially blocked the passage higher up, it was an easy gradient to the top of the escarpment.

Loose sand had drifted down into this natural funnel; in places it looked soft and deep enough to cause problems for the heavy vehicle.

The tribesman rattled his handcuffs. "Free me, *sah'b*—I will walk ahead of you. It will be safer."

Bolan hesitated.

"I cannot outrun your bullets," the bedu said, indicating the Uzi. "I can find the best path to follow."

Bolan unlocked the cuffs. Danny wondered why he seemed so reluctant; it sounded like a good idea to her. The man climbed down, carefully scanning the ground as he plodded up the wind-cut passageway.

The Hog sat there idling while Bolan modified the Uzi.

The man turned, beckoning them forward with a wave. He moved faster now, the hill was getting easier, until he skipped sideways with several nimble steps.

Bolan was already halfway up the slope when the nomad made that last odd crablike maneuver. He pulled up hard, jamming on the hand brake.

With utter horror Danny suddenly realized why Bolan had been so apprehensive. Not four feet from the right front tire, the shifting wind had blown back enough sand to reveal a dark metal lump! The desert thief had led them straight into a mine trap.

13

"Stop right there!" Bolan commanded.

The man glanced back as Bolan stood up—and as the American's hands cleared the windshield, he saw the fat round barrel of the silencer affixed to the Uzi.

The Arab weighed his chances. He was safely out of the mine strip. That big flat rock offered him cover less than twenty feet away.

Bolan did not give him the chance to try for it . . . a short burst stuttered softly from the submachine gun. The whining bullets made more noise as they ricocheted off the corner of the slab, chipping out puffs of powdered rock.

The chief knew he'd never make it in one piece. The American would cut him in two.

"Get back down here!" Bolan ordered gruffly. "Now!"

He handed the gun to Danny. "Watch that trickster." Then he turned to a box in the back and opened the lid, pulling out what he'd claimed to the customs officer was a metal detector. Danny knew now that he hadn't lied exactly—he just hadn't told the whole truth.

The device was a metal detector of sorts: a highly efficient, compact unit for sweeping mines. Bolan tested the ground alongside the Hog before stepping down. He was waiting in front of the Jeep when the crafty nomad finally got back to them.

"One more false move and she's going to pull the trigger, you understand?"

The man nodded vigorously.

"Now I'm going ahead to sweep a way clear for the Jeep."

Another jerk of his head.

"I'll call out where they are…and you, my friend," said Bolan, handing him a wooden stake, "are going to dig them up."

The bedu's throat bobbed with a terrified swallow.

Bolan moved methodically upward, listening through the lightweight headset and watching the gauge as he swung the detector in a smooth short arc. Twelve paces out and he stopped, pointing to the ground a few inches from his left boot. "Okay, do it!"

The man, trying to stop his hands from shaking, prodded gingerly at the soil.

"Don't try anything stupid," Bolan snarled as he continued to walk up the slope, sweeping a pattern wide enough to take the Hog through safely.

Danny's brow and upper lip were beaded with perspiration and it wasn't just from the early-morning sun that was beginning to arc behind them. She held her breath each time Mack paused, his feet remaining stock-still, as he marked the location of the next mine.

It took nearly fifty minutes to clear a way to the spot where the big block cut the passage to half. Bolan eyed the boulder, the slope beneath and all the other details as he contemplated turning things to his advantage. Prodding the man in the back, they retraced their footsteps to the Hog.

"Okay, Danny, cross your fingers and hope we did it right."

Keeping his eye fixed on the critical path, Bolan gunned the motor and the Jeep shot up the slope. He got out of the vehicle, indicating the double-crossing native should do the same. Then he turned to Danny and said, "Take the Hog almost to the top, but stay below the skyline. Then cover it with the net and wait for me there."

"What are you going to do?"

Bolan picked up the silenced Uzi and pointed at the prisoner. "He's going to put all those mines back in the sand again, but in different places."

DANICA JONES WAS NOT A SMOKER, not anymore. She'd quit a long time ago. But right at this moment she would gladly have lit up a cigarette.

The unexpected violence of last night and the strain of the past hour had left her with the shakes inside. But I asked for it, Danny reminded herself, I wanted it this way...being close to death is the cost of feeling so fully alive.

It was another half hour before Bolan reappeared. He marched up the hill alone. For a minute she thought he might have let that wily bastard go, even though she knew in her heart what must have happened back there.

"He should have kept his word to us," was all the explanation Bolan offered her. "He swore on his honor."

Together they walked to the top of the slope, crouching low as they slipped over the ridge. They had a panoramic view of Khurabi's Forbidden Zone stretched out below them.

The actual distance down the far side of the Jebel Kharg was greater than what they'd climbed up to get here, but the slope descended less steeply.

Camels, traders and their miserable human cargo of slaves had, over so many years, beaten a track that was easy to follow. It cut across the hillside diagonally, disappearing through a forest of sandstone boulders, then dipped through a ravine leading all the way down to the desert floor beyond.

Sand, millions of tons of it blown from the Empty Quarter, washed up here like rolling waves upon ancient shores of the Jebel Kharg.

Bolan said nothing as he searched the terrain sector by sector.

Far away to their right, sunlight twinkled briefly on the windshield of a car or truck using Khurabi's only interior highway; but even through his powerful binoculars it was nothing more than a momentary flash.

The road, which Grimaldi had picked as the only feasible landing site, squeezed past the terminal shoulder of the jebel and the oil fields ranged along the frontier. It was a natural bottleneck that would be watched night and day. Bolan knew he was right to have chosen the more difficult track into this inaccessible region, despite the problems they had run into on the way.

He scanned left slowly, looking for any movement or sign of the patrols that Hassan was bound to have dispatched. The desert lay absolutely still, waiting to be hammered by the full force of the midday sun.

Finally, slightly to the left of their present position, he focused on a small irregularity poking up amid the distant dunes.

"Take a look over there," he told Danny, handing her the field glasses. "Hagadan? Is that the fortress?"

"It's in the right spot. How far off would you say that is?"

"Oh, twenty miles at least." Bolan dusted himself off. "Let's get going. We've got a lot of ground to cover."

Only when she turned back, squinting into the harsh glare, did Danny fully appreciate the wisdom of Bolan's wilderness route to Hagadan. From this angle the sun would be rising behind them all morning. Prying eyes would not choose to look directly along their line of approach.

Bolan stripped off the camouflage covering and left Danny to repack it. He rearranged the gear in the back of the Hog, opening the long wooden crate and lifting out the M-60.

Chandler had engineered a special mount for the machine gun. It took Bolan only a few moments to slot the support column into its base. Danny wondered what that nosy customs officer would have said...there was no disguising their intentions now: they were going off to war.

They were halfway down the far side of the jebel when Bolan started talking. "I won't kill a man merely because of what he believes in. Even if I think he's misguided, perverse or just plain mad, that's his affair."

The suddenness with which Bolan launched into these reflections of his past life certainly surprised Danica Jones. But she remained silent.

"But when a person, an organization or even a country starts to cause havoc in the name of those beliefs—when they torture anyone who doesn't happen to agree with them, maim the children, murder the innocent—that's when they become the enemies of decency, order and humanity. And that's when they become my enemies, too."

Danny listened carefully. He did not seem to be offering her any excuses or simply trying to justify what had happened in the past few hours; rather she sensed that he needed to paint an overall picture for her. He was letting her know more precisely what she was involved in. And why he tried to help others despite the incredible risks to his own life.

"I will defend myself, those I care for and the values of freedom—I'll defend them to the death!" This was not a hollow boast but a plain statement of fact. "I took no pleasure in killing those guys back there. I admire the bedu. But that man and his sons were double-crossing thieves who intended to murder us. Like I said—he called the play and made it 'them or us.'"

He paused to navigate between two jagged outcrops.

"I didn't come here to Khurabi because I hate Islam and think it should be put down. I don't. There are many things worthy of deep and abiding respect in

the Muslim world. The Koran sets out a harsh code—
not one that I could easily live by—but if a man wishes
to follow it in peace, okay, then I wish him luck...."

Bolan's eyes had a distant look. Was he scanning for
trouble ahead of them? Or was he remembering another time, another place, another battle?

"Some of the bravest men I ever had the privilege
of fighting alongside were Tarik Khan and his *muja-
hedeen* in the mountains of Afghanistan. No, I won't
go on a mission, knowing that men will probably die,
just because they worship Allah."

He glanced across at her. Danny gazed back into
those pale blue eyes, awed by the strength of his com-
mitment as she now perceived the broader perspec-
tives of the Executioner's endless war.

"There was a journalist once, back in Nam, who
tried to write me up as some sort of commie-hating
psychotic. Well, I don't hate anyone for merely be-
lieving in Marx or Lenin—although, considering their
theories have been thoroughly discredited by the events
of this century, I'd certainly have to say their faith was
misplaced."

Danny had to smile at this last remark. She'd come
across several true believers in the Marxist-Leninist
line at university. She had heard otherwise intelligent
professors, often indulging in the most affluent of life-
styles, mouthing all the usual platitudes of commu-
nist brotherhood. Her thoughts were interrupted as
Bolan continued.

"But it's in the name of those same beliefs—even
masquerading them as a scientific theory—that the
Soviets have murdered, what, thirty or forty million

people . . . in their war to first seize power, by a deliberate policy of famine, in slave labor camps, in the treacherous way they conducted themselves both with and then against Hitler, through surrogate terrorist armies, and now with the rape of Afghanistan . . . The list of their atrocities is endless.

"But their goal is simple: they have to dominate the whole world. They've warned us on enough occasions that that's what they're up to—it's our own fault if we don't listen. And that's what makes the Soviets, not the ordinary Russian man in the street, my enemies. Particularly the KGB. I oppose them because of the horror they inflict in the name of their outmoded beliefs."

Danny recalled the nightmare scenes she had witnessed in Southeast Asia and knew that in his worldwide campaigns Bolan must have seen ten times worse.

"It's the same now with Hassan Zayoud. I don't care if he kneels five times a day toward Mecca. It has always seemed obvious to me that this power, this universal life force we call God must, by definition, be beyond our own limited comprehension."

"Of course," agreed Danny. The detailed study she had made of the past had led her to much the same conclusion. "I'm sure that the great religions are all worshiping different facets of the same limitless source—each formulating their faith in different ways."

"Exactly," said Bolan. "But Zayoud wants to be the new Sword of Islam, spreading his personal beliefs in a bloody Crescent Revolution—and to do that he'll kidnap kids or gather an army of hired killers, build a bomb or murder his own brother, given half a chance. When he ordered his men to snatch Kevin Baker in Florida, Hassan Zayoud called down a sentence upon himself with that action. That's where I come in.... Hey, talking of enemy troops, look at that dust!''

''They're coming this way,'' said Danny. ''Quick, over there . . . we can hide behind those rocks.''

Bolan slipped the Hog into the depression behind the boulders. They were less than two hundred yards from the edge of the sand and still slightly above it. The long sweeping crest of the nearest dune had protected them for the few vital moments that were needed to reach safe cover. A Jeep with four men aboard clambered into view and rolled down the banked sand.

The driver, in a khaki shirt and red-checkered burnoose, was one of Hassan's troopers, as was the man who sat next to him; the two guys in the back were mercenaries. They were carrying Uzis, too—the weapons had been on Ruark's ''shopping list.'' Bolan recognized the bullet-headed giant with tattooed forearms as Bull Keegan.

Danny held her breath, wondering if the new arrivals were going to inspect the trail down from the jebel. Bolan took his gun off safety. He was taking no chances.

The Arab jumped out of the passenger seat and cast around for a sign, while Keegan checked the bottom edge of the hillside through glasses.

Bolan and his companion were close enough to pick up the conversation. ''Waste of goddamn time coming out here. C'mon, let's get back and find some shade," Bull Keegan said.

Zayoud's men hopped back inside. The driver let out the clutch too quickly, jerking forward before stalling in a pothole. It almost threw Keegan overboard. He started berating the driver. "You stupid...haven't you learned anything? Jeez, your boss figures he's going to take over the country with dumb bastards like you to back him? Huh, I dunno...Jim, you take the wheel."

The other merc climbed down into the driver's seat. They pulled away with Keegan still swearing at the native soldier until they were out of earshot.

The Jeep vanished through a dip between two massive dunes and soon even the sound of the engine died away.

"That," said Danny, "was uncomfortably close."

"Best thing that could have happened," Bolan contradicted her. She looked at him curiously. "We'll give them twenty minutes' head start," he explained, "then follow them back to the fortress."

14

Bolan noticed that the desert floor of the Forbidden Zone was not quite the uniform sea of sand that it had first seemed from the craggy heights behind them.

For many square miles the unimpeded wind had indeed built up great transverse dunes—frozen waves in a burning ocean—but there were harder patches, too, and here the sand had been pushed into the crescent shapes of *barchan* dunes, all neatly pointing downwind. In other places the desert had been stripped to almost naked rock.

With utmost caution Bolan followed the scouting patrol toward the target. He and Danny paused often, the Hog's hull down behind a crest, waiting for the right moment to slip safely across. Once, they spotted Keegan waving his fist as he ripped into Zayoud's men for their stupidity.

The sun climbed toward its zenith. Danny used a towel to fashion a head cloth to protect herself. It was not unendurably sticky; out here perspiration simply evaporated as soon as it appeared.

They had stopped for a water break when Bolan spotted a truck approaching from the right. It rendezvoused with Keegan's Jeep and, after a brief conference, the two vehicles proceeded in convoy back to

the base. The double tracks were easy enough to follow.

Bolan memorized what markers he could in this re-
petitive landscape: once it was a peculiar star-shaped
dune, and in another spot he noted a rust-colored
rock; often he glanced back to take his bearings from
the notch they had crossed atop the jebel.

The powerful 600 horsepower V8 engine that
Chandler had fitted in the Sand Hog throbbed quietly
as it propelled them over the shifting terrain. Bolan
checked his watch frequently against the speedometer
and odometer.

"Stay here," he finally instructed Danny, and
stalked up the slope ahead to double-check their position. He remained there some time. When he came
back he told Danny, "We'll have to go very carefully
now . . . we're almost there."

Her pulse was racing with excitement but Danny
was determined not to let it show. She wondered if
Mack felt anything at having got this far, for being so
dangerously near Zayoud's headquarters? If he did,
it didn't show; he seemed so calm and self-assured.

Bolan turned more to the south for this final leg,
leaving the churned-up tracks of the patrol vehicles, as
they kept low in a long trough behind another golden
barricade of sand. There was a barren ridge of rock
beyond it, cracked by the brutal elements and sculpted
into a labyrinth of weirdly shaped protrusions.

He drew in beneath the shadowy underside of a
giant stone mushroom, parking tight against the wind-
scoured pillar.

"This should be safe enough," he said, switching off the engine, then adding realistically, "well, as safe as anywhere around here can be. First things first, let's rig the netting, then wipe out our tracks."

There was little sign of their presence on the hard rock surface. Danny scuffed out a tire track in one softer patch of grit. When she turned toward the formation where they were parked, she had to look twice to find the hiding place. It was amazing how well the camouflaged Hog had melded into the surroundings.

She knew she was going to be left here alone, perhaps for many hours, once Mack set off for the fortress. But her concern for his safety now outweighed her own fears.

"Let's take a look at the castle," said Bolan. He led the way up a narrow cleft to the top of the sandstone ridge.

Danny was staggered at how frighteningly close they were to the fortress.

"It's impressive," Danny breathed.

"And damn near impregnable," added Bolan.

In their present position they were less than half a mile from the southeastern corner of the fortifications. The dunes, smaller here and studded with rocks, swirled right to the base of the massive upthrust on which Hagadan was built.

The rugged cliffs, covered in places with a tangle of thorn bushes, reared up for a hundred feet or more and then the thick stone walls, still in remarkably good repair, rose for another fifty feet above the foundation line.

To their left they could see that a single gravel track rose along an approach ramp directly beneath the battlements. At the top of the incline it twisted in an L-turn through the main gateway. Four guards, all carrying modern rifles, stood on duty at this entrance.

There were more soldiers stationed on the rooftops of the square towers that marked the corners of the fortress. Two more round towers and the central keep stood proudly within the protection of these stout outer walls.

Bolan surveyed the crenellated towers—there must have been at least thirty men on watch, and those were only the ones he could count from this angle. How many sentries would be on duty at night? And how watchful would they be?

The binoculars were fitted with extended rubber shields to mask off any reflections but Bolan still instinctively lowered them for a moment when a small party suddenly appeared on top of the keep.

"Is that Zayoud?" asked Danny.

"Yeah, that's him all right." He gave her the glasses. "And look who he's got with him!"

There was no mistaking the young boy who stood by Hassan Zayoud. The circular image that Danny focused on was a smaller replica of the locket Bolan had shown her when they first met. The suntanned youth pointing off into the distance behind them was Kevin Baker.

Zayoud, with his neatly trimmed black beard and glittering eyes, extended his arm upon which was perched a sleek falcon. He removed the hood, untied the tethering thong and launched the bird above the tower. With strong, steady strokes it rose high above the desert, then glided silently over the rocks that concealed Bolan and Danny.

It swooped, regained altitude and then plunged like a dive bomber on some unseen prey. When it rose into view again, it was carrying the small limp body of some desert creature clutched in its talons. Returning to the tower seemed to take a greater effort as the bird flew quite low over their heads.

"Good thing birds can't talk," said Bolan.

Kevin applauded the return of the successful hunter. And Zayoud was pleased with his prized bird's performance. He had spent many hours training it to attack men as well as smaller, more natural prey. But something else had attracted the sheikh's attention....

Danny nudged Bolan's arm: a squad of Zayoud's handpicked guards was being marched up the approach road. Craig Harrison was in command of the detail. They looked hot and dusty. He must have been putting them through some grueling paces.

"Keep your eyes open for anyone else." Bolan raised the glasses and began a detailed examination of every inch along the cliffs below the wall, assessing each fissure, each spur, each overhang as if his life depended on it...because, before this night was over, he knew it would.

SOMEWHERE, FAR OUT in the silvery phantom shadows of the desert night, a jackal cried for its mate. The mournful sound echoed on the midnight air.

Bolan padded forward—another hunter on the prowl—slipping from the cover of a boulder, then seeking the shelter of the scrub that lined the shallow ditch surrounding the rock of Hagadan. The ancient fortress now loomed above him, the walls glowing ghostly pale and blotting out the heavens.

His pack was heavy with specially prepared explosives, and spare mags for the Uzi were carried in long pockets at the sides of his trousers. A rope was coiled around his shoulder, and he carried a padded grapnel in his left hand.

The hook came in handy to steady himself as he mounted the steep slope at the bottom of the cliff. There were small fans of loose scree in places. Every handhold had to be tested; every footstep carefully planted.

Bolan followed the rough outline of the ascent route he had picked out earlier that afternoon. He came to the first overhang. It was tougher than it had looked through the glasses; perhaps he could squeeze past this obstacle at the far end.

He continued to traverse, reaching out to grab hold of the wizened shrub growing in a crack beyond the ledge he was balanced on. His fingers circled the tough stem and Bolan pulled himself along.

There was a fissure in the rock face that he climbed for thirty feet. He had almost cleared the top of this natural chimney when his hand dislodged a loose pebble. It dropped away into the darkness.

Bolan remained frozen where he was.

The small stone landed in the sand below with a dull thunk. He waited for a sentry to stick his head over the battlements.

Nothing.

No one had been alarmed.

Nearing the top of the cliff he saw the faint trace of a match end being flicked carelessly from the wall. Again he waited, hands straining to hold himself tight against the cliff, wondering if the smoker would casually lean over the edge and glance down. He stayed in position longer this time. Every second was increasing the strain.

Bolan reached the final bulging lip of granite below the huge foundation stones. This, too, had been deceptive. He weighed his chances of making it with the hefty pack in place. They didn't look good. If he failed to pull himself up and over on the first attempt, the pack would sure as hell drag him down. And it was a long drop to the bottom.

This called for some delicate maneuvering. First, he shrugged the coil from his shoulder. Then, bracing his feet, he freed his hand long enough to secure the end of the rope to the rucksack shoulder strap. The pack had a special quick release that freed it from his back.

There was a spot over to his right, a small shelf wide enough to balance the load. Bolan set it down.

With one palm pressing firmly on the ceiling of stone above his head, Bolan stretched back with the other arm and felt for a hold with the grapnel. It took three tries to find a narrow chink in which to jam one point of the triple hook.

Bolan pulled hard on the shank. It seemed secure, but there was only one way to really test it and he could not put it off.

He transferred his weight, jumping out from the ledge. His other hand smacked against the rock, fingers scrabbling to find that second hold.

His bleeding fingertips closed round a granite knob and he levered himself bodily around the overhang. There was an uneven ledge, about a foot wide, at the very bottom of the wall. Bolan lay there resting sideways for a moment, then he pulled the bag up after him.

As he straightened up, a screeching, flapping ball of feathers and claws struck him on the forehead. He was slapped across the nose as the startled bird beat its wings in a frantic attempt to scare off the intruder.

Bolan brushed it aside; and with a final indignant squawk, the bird flew off to find another perch. He wasn't sure who had been more surprised—him or the sleeping bird.

Leaving the pack secured to the end of the rope, Bolan relooped the line, leaving a long leader free for the swing it was going to take.

The pendulum made a faint whoosh with every pass. Bolan twirled it completely and let go.

This was the worst moment; the biggest risk of all. And he had no choice but to take it.

The hooks and shank were sheathed with high-density foam sleeves. The grapnel made little sound as it lodged in a gun port high above Bolan's head.

He tugged on the rope. The tips were trapped on the sill up there. Bolan gradually increased the pressure of his test pull . . . still it held.

He glanced back once at the desert—out to where Danny was hiding with the Hog—then up he went, hand over hand, rubber-soled boots walking up the weathered facing. His muscles ached from the effort required to pull himself and the added weight of the equipment he carried up the wall.

Bolan was almost two-thirds the way to his goal, perhaps at the forty-foot mark, when he heard someone chuckle behind the window slit slightly to his left. The murmur of small talk drifted indistinctly by him. It was riskier to hang there dangling by a thread than to proceed. Bolan hauled himself up the rest of the way.

He wriggled through the defenders' firing slot and huddled close to the wall, catching his breath and his bearings at the same time.

The nightstalker was on a flagstone walkway, repaired in places with wooden planking, about twenty feet from the nearest corner tower. A lookout up there was stamping his feet to stay awake and ward off the chilly night breeze.

Bolan wiped the sweat from his forehead, crawled back into the man-size slit and dragged up the rucksack.

He lugged the loaded pack across the stonework. A few small chips, broken off by the point of the grapnel hook, were swept back off the ledge. They hit the walkway with a rattle.

Bolan heard the sound of boots on the worn stone steps within the tower. He pushed the pack against the wall and bundled the rope behind it.

The door at the end opened with a creak. Dim lighting from inside briefly streaked the flagstones as the Arab guard stepped out into the cool air.

He took a deep breath, then stepped forward, puzzled to find one of the foreign soldiers up here on duty.

Bolan waited, outwardly casual but internally poised to spring, until he noticed the trooper stare curiously past his legs. He'd seen the pack.... The man twisted to unsling his rifle.

Before he could shout a warning, Bolan was upon him with the silent ferocity of a nocturnal predator. He clamped a hand tight across the Arab's mouth, swung him around and smashed the sentry into the low wall. Apart from the grunt of suddenly expelled air, the man was too winded to call out for his comrades.

The Executioner cracked the guy's skull hard against the inside edge of the battlements. The senseless guard released his grip on the rifle. Bolan set down the weapon quietly, lifted the body to the slit and shoved it into space.

There was no scream before the man's broken body struck a soft patch of sand a hundred fifty feet below.

The guard's burnoose had fallen off in the brief one-sided scuffle. Bolan scooped it up and put it on, now disguised like some of the other mercs he'd seen. He moved the bag into the deepest shadows behind the door.

He had barely got the gear hidden from obvious view when he heard the sound of footsteps quickly mounting the tower staircase. Bolan picked up the rifle and was leaning nonchalantly on the wall when the second man appeared, still puffing from the climb.

"Thought I heard something...." There was a lazy Southern drawl in the newcomer's voice. He was one of Ruark's men.

"Yes, so did I," said Bolan. "But there's nothing happening. These old places give me the creeps."

"Yeah, you can say that again. Give me the bush any day." Sounded like this guy had seen action in Africa.

Bolan pulled the cigarettes from his pocket. He offered one to the Southerner. They lit up and Bolan knew the other man was watching him over cupped hands. He was counting on the fact that there were too many mercs, with fresh recruits still arriving, for himself to be recognized as an outsider.

"Haven't seen you before—you come with that mob yesterday?"

"Nah, the one before that." The guy might be testing him: maybe nobody came yesterday. Bolan needed an identity he could use and fast. He picked the name of a dead man, a merc he knew had got killed in a former mission to Africa. "Scarr's my name. Brendan Scarr."

"Billy Joe Hooker—that's me. You're here just in time for the shooting match. Keegan reckons we'll be on the move within forty-eight hours."

"Yeah, well, what does Bull know? Ruark's calling the shots on this contract and I'll wait till I hear him say it," bluffed Bolan.

"Right. Still, I'll be glad to get out of this oven," said Hooker. He glanced back over his shoulder. "I'd better check the tower. Those boys are probably asleep up there."

Hooker did not notice the pack lying in the corner as he slipped back through the doorway.

Bolan ground out the butt beneath his heel. It was time for the one-man strike force to sow a few seeds of destruction.

15

Bolan lingered in the shadows, listening to Billy Joe Hooker running up the final flight of stairs. He could hear the muffled chitchat as the merc passed the time of night with the soldiers on duty up there. Bolan stayed motionless as two small figures crossed the courtyard below.

He had to get off these narrow walkways, where at any moment he might be challenged by somebody more suspicious of him than that Southern kid.

Moving now, he passed through the empty upper chamber of the southeastern tower complex and moved swiftly along the top of the adjacent stretch of wall until he reached the next corner tower.

The door was standing ajar. Bolan ducked inside and saw that this top story was as deserted as the last one. The wooden trapdoor in the ceiling was wide open. The sentry snuffled as he dozed at his post.

The second step down was chipped and loose. Bolan pulled the slab back carefully and, after setting the digital timer for 0930 hours, he slipped the first deadly package into the hollow underneath and replaced the cracked step.

He could not risk wiring the main gate. The guards there were bound to be more alert, even at night, so he couldn't place another charge. But, more importantly, if the slightest thing went wrong with his timing, if he had not gotten hold of Kevin by zero hour, then the explosion would end up sealing him inside the castle, rather than stalling the pursuit.

This tower, the one he was now in, was the most important one to blow, for it directly covered the ramp road below it. With the first charge in place, Bolan quickly descended the steps into the courtyard. He hugged a darkened patch by the wall, squeezing in behind a Jeep to survey the new dangers that faced him.

The cleanest hit would have been to snatch Kevin while the boy was asleep and spirit him out of Hagadan. Zayoud was not about to make it that easy for him. The main doors leading into the central keep were floodlit and Bolan could see two big mercs lounging on the steps outside. And they were flanked by four more of the sheikh's own bodyguards.

Bolan knew there would be more trusted men stationed right outside the sleeping quarters. He decided the inner sanctum was effectively barred to him. He could not risk a shooting match with Kevin stuck in the middle. Bolan figured he'd have to wait for the boy to come outside. However, Bolan could still use the remaining hours of darkness to his own purpose...these guys were going to think they were being hit by an artillery barrage!

Zayoud himself could be counted on to be awake for prayers at sunrise. As Bolan attached a smaller charge, set for 0932, to the underside of the Jeep, he hoped the Baker boy wasn't planning on sleeping in.

The Executioner checked around the long courtyard for the next target of opportunity.

A radio mast sprouted from the top of the northwestern tower, the corner of the fortress Bolan could not see clearly from his earlier vantage point among the rocks. Too risky. Three men were posted outside the lower entrance, and the guys upstairs were wide awake—at least, slivers of bright light showed through the slit windows near the top. And he could hear the chugging sound of a generator in that direction.

Two things were of paramount importance to him now: transport and ammunition.

At the far end of the yard, the motor-pool sergeant and a couple of his men were still servicing a dark green Land Rover; it had to be Zayoud's own car for them to be working this late. A row of six trucks were parked neatly in line against the courtyard wall. Two half-tracks and four more Jeeps were aligned at right angles to the other vehicles. The naked bulbs of the work lamps lit the whole area at that end with a harsh yellow glare, which would spotlight Bolan carrying the bulky rucksack.

Two more wooden sheds had been built against the inner wall, about thirty feet farther along from where he was hidden. The first structure was a stable—Bolan could tell by the slightly pungent odor carried on the breeze. He slipped into the narrow alley between the two buildings.

The outer shack, with a tar-paper roof, had a small back door hidden from the view of the guards inside the compound. It was padlocked. Bolan removed the multitool from his belt and unscrewed the clasp. The huge stone walls of Hagadan gave a completely false sense of security to the troops boxed up inside.

Bolan gently pushed the door inward.

The place was stacked from floor to roof with well-marked crates: there were smoke grenades, frags and incendiaries; boxes of 7.62 mm ammunition, 9 mm and even some old British .303s; feed belts and a couple of mortars; half a dozen containers stenciled in Russian held greased AK-47s. Everything Zayoud needed to launch his treacherous coup. And Bolan's actions had forced his hand—he had to strike soon or lose any advantage of surprise.

Bolan left three more charges strategically placed deep within the ammo dump. He timed them all for 0933. He was locking himself into a tight schedule.

He shut the door and replaced the clasp. A loose plank in the side of the stable gave him access to the hiding place he needed.

The big white stallion, the one he had seen in the satellite photographs, snickered softly in the shadows.

Bolan stood at the end of his stall and whispered, "Easy, boy." The horse quieted down.

Bolan tested the ladder for noise, then climbed into the warm scented darkness beneath the sloping roof. Within moments both he and the stallion were resting easily.

BOLAN AWOKE, REFRESHED, before the native troops began their early-morning prayer ritual.

A couple of trucks went out, followed by Harrison standing in the back of a Jeep. Bolan watched the patrols leaving and scanned the yard through a knothole under the eaves of the hayloft.

Zayoud strode over to the communication center, snapping orders at various men he passed.

There was a shouted commotion from atop the southeastern tower. Someone had spotted the guard's body from the parapet. A squad ran down toward the main gate, detailed to check out what had happened to the man.

Hassan Zayoud reappeared, disturbed by the sudden confusion. Impatiently he tapped a leather riding crop against his leg, waiting for the report on the sentry.

Bolan heard footsteps close by. Bull Keegan and Billy Joe Hooker, still rubbing the sleep from his eyes, paused by the stable wall. They had no idea that the guard's attacker was only a few feet above them listening to every word.

"Probably fell off the wall," commented Keegan, with a derisive snort. "They're all a bunch of jerks. Still, nothing's going to stop Zayoud now. We're parading at 1630 and going in tonight. By tomorrow afternoon there'll be a new king."

"Yeah," said Billy Joe Hooker, "then I'm going to find me one of those A-rab chicks and look at what they've been hiding under those veils. If I like what I see, I'm gonna have a little fun with her on the spot."

"And if you don't?"

"I'll tie the veil back on and have her anyway!" said Billy Joe, laughing.

"Uh-oh, here comes Zayoud. Let's get scarce or he'll be ordering the lot of us out on another patrol...."

"Where's Captain Ruark?" snapped the prince.

Captain now, thought Bolan. Ruark never made it past sergeant last he heard.

Keegan doubled away smartly to find the mercenary commander. Billy Joe Hooker sidled off in the other direction to avoid being picked for patrol duty.

There was movement all over the yard. The mechanics were giving each vehicle a final inspection. A bunch of recently arrived mercs were gathered round a blackboard, being tested on the layout of the city and their target assignments. The court falconer was talking quietly to his hooded charges.

Bolan crept down from the loft.

The main gates were being dragged wide open. A convoy of six more trucks, plus two Saracen armored cars, rolled into the fortress. The squad, carrying the ambushed sentry's remains, staggered in behind the new vehicles.

Bolan took advantage of all this activity. He waited till the passing trucks effectively blocked any view of the stable, then confidently walked out into the morning sunlight. A couple of Arab recruits to Zayoud's cause sat nearby listening to a third soldier lecture them on stripping a Bren. The corporal seemed to be stuck....

"Try the body-locking pin next," suggested Bolan brightly. Within moments the stranger was showing them the finer points of field-stripping the sturdy

British weapon—just one more merc passing on his trade.

A crowd came spilling out down the steps of the main complex—chow time was over. One of Zayoud's shiny-eyed devotees saw the lookout's body and began wailing in grief. The sheikh himself had gone over to inspect the battered corpse and now had some very pointed questions for Ruark.

Another Arab trooper came across to join Bolan's informal lecture group. He interrupted them with the news that their comrade certainly had not been shot or stabbed.

The American shrugged and redirected their attention to the light machine gun. "Okay, like I was saying, you've got to watch the gas gauge. That's this knob here...."

Ruark had called a couple of his men over and was grilling them in front of Zayoud. Bolan's hand never strayed more than a few inches from the Uzi, which he had placed on the corner of the groundsheet.

He showed no particular interest when Kevin skipped down into the courtyard. The boy waited by Zayoud's elbow until the prince glanced around with an impatient greeting.

Bolan was too far away to hear their brief conversation, but he did see the sheikh wave toward the stable with a distracted gesture of approval.

Kevin crossed to the wooden shed almost at a trot, as if he were trying to get there before Zayoud could change his mind.

Bolan returned his attention to the trainees. "Right, now see if you can do it without any help from me.

Come on, you can unscrew the barrel faster than
that—it won't break off in your hand!''

He rose from a half-crouching position and by pre-
tending to watch the men working on the gun from a
different angle, he moved around for a better view of
the yard.

Kevin led the stallion out from the stable. He was a
magnificent horse—not pure white, after all, but more
of a silvery gray—with wide nostrils and intelligent
eyes. His rippling muscles bespoke the speed and
stamina of the finest Arabian stock. The youngster
gave just the slightest twitch to encourage the horse to
follow him around the perimeter.

The sheikh had left Ruark to interrogate more of his
men.

''Just walk him for a while,'' he instructed Kevin.
Then Zayoud turned in Bolan's direction. ''You—
come here!''

Bolan was not sure he had been the one Zayoud was
addressing. He saw Billy Joe Hooker tapping his
chest, an inquiring look on his face.

''Yes, you'll do!'' barked the sheikh. ''Stay with the
boy while he exercises my horse.'' Then Zayoud
stalked back up the slope to see if Ruark was any
nearer solving the mystery of the guard's violent de-
mise.

''It's okay, Billy Joe, I'm finished here. I'll look
after the boy,'' Bolan assured him. ''You find some
place to catch up on your beauty sleep. We're going to
need to be rested up before tonight.''

"Thanks, Scarr." Hooker gave him a sly grin and wandered off to leave "Brendan Scarr" on kiddie patrol.

Bolan caught up with the teenager. "Expensive-looking horse, what's he worth? A million for stud?"

"Malik's worth a lot more than that!" scoffed Kevin.

He did not seem to be unduly uncomfortable or under great stress. His jeans were freshly laundered, his short-sleeved shirt was neat and he wore a new pair of running shoes. The boy looked healthy and well cared for—and not at all like someone being held against his will.

Bolan ambled alongside, considering his next move very carefully. Time was running out....

"Are you an American?" asked Kevin out of idle curiosity. It was just something to say, he didn't seem to be especially homesick.

"Yeah...at least, that's what it says on my passport," replied Bolan, still playing the battle-weary merc.

"These guys are from all over the world, quite a few from England."

"Well, we're paid to be here," said Bolan. "But what are you doing so far from home? Shouldn't you be in school someplace?"

Kevin shrugged. It was something he did not want to talk about.

Bolan risked pushing the point. "Are you in some kind of trouble?"

"Why do you ask that?" shot back Kevin. "Are you?"

"Yes, kind of..."

Kevin was looking down at the sand when he said quietly, "So am I...sort of...but that's, well, that's all behind me now."

They had passed the communications center and were halfway along the north wall. No one was in earshot. Bolan made sure of that before he told the boy, "No, Kevin, it isn't all over, but you can face up to it. You can still wipe the slate clean."

The youngster stopped in his tracks at the mention of his name. There was something firm yet truthful in the stranger's tone.

Bolan fished out Mrs. Baker's locket. "Your mother gave me this, Chip."

"My parents sent you to take me back?"

"No, Chip, they didn't. But I have come a long way to ask you to return home."

Kevin shook his head in disbelief. He was very wary now. "Hassan said that someone would try to get through."

Bolan stopped to pet Malik behind the ears. He could only hope their conversation appeared innocent enough to any onlookers. "Do you know what you're involved in here?"

"I know what I got out of..." There was a stubborn streak in Kevin that was starting to spell trouble. Bolan knew how willful a teenager could be—it made him think of his younger brother, Johnny. Kevin remained moodily defiant. "Look, they were going to stick me in jail."

"This isn't much better than a prison, is it?" Bolan challenged him. It was obvious that Zayoud had played skillfully on the boy's emotions.

He had to keep Kevin talking, and yet not say anything that would trigger the boy into shouting an alarm for help. Zayoud was on the opposite side of the yard speaking with his falconer.

"No, that isn't true." The youth's protest was overemphatic; maybe he was trying to convince himself as much as the man who had come to retrieve him. "Hassan's been great to me. He's given me anything I've asked for. I'm going to have my own computer lab soon."

Yeah, thought Bolan, after a lot of blood has been spilled on the streets of Khurabi.

"Didn't your parents look after you?"

"Huh, the only talks I had with my father were about grades, and how I had to do better each time. He'd pull out a checkbook to reward me for my marks. And Mom...well, I never could talk to her. She never understood any of the things that I was involved in. Hassan's different—he's really interested in what I can do...."

As the boy talked on, defending Zayoud, Bolan realized what he was up against: the sheikh had offered Kevin the one thing he had never received from his parents or his classmates—a seemingly unequivocal and, so far at least, undemanding friendship.

What young hacker could resist the lure of his own computer setup, no expenses spared? What other kid could play around with an Arabian stallion or a trained hawk? What teenager wouldn't love to be treated like a young prince?

Bolan suddenly doubted that Kevin even knew the truth about what had happened on that fateful, fatal morning in Florida. According to the police report, the boy had been bundled into the getaway car before the escorting officers were massacred. What other lies had Zayoud told him?

Further discussion was academic. The numerals on Bolan's watch flickered past 0926. They were fifty yards from the open gate. Bolan had to make his play, now!

He did not get the chance.

The next move was made for him....

16

"Scarr!" Ruark bellowed from the steps. Billy Joe Hooker was standing next to him, still pointing toward Bolan. "Hey, you, Brendan Scarr! Isn't that what you call yourself?"

Several rifles were turned in their direction. Zayoud was fondling his hawk. He spun, startled by Ruark's challenge, and raised his free hand to stop any hasty action.

"I don't believe you, Brendan Scarr." Ruark spit out the name with a sarcastic flourish. "I say you're a liar. I heard Scarr got hisself killed somewhere in Africa. But maybe you know more about that than me...."

Bolan held his hand firm on Kevin's shoulder. He was in a double bind. There was no way he would ever use a kid as hostage for his own safety, but he did not want Kevin running blindly into a cross fire.

The commotion in the courtyard had caught the attention of the sentries strung out along the parapets. Bolan, the boy and the horse now stood at the focal point of more than forty guns.

Zayoud issued a harsh command to his feathered prize. The gyrfalcon swooped forward as the sheikh commanded, "Kill!"

The bird was halfway across the open space, streaking toward Bolan's face, when the big man reluctantly squeezed the trigger. He fired a short burst from the hip.

One hundred thousand dollars worth of rare bird was instantly shredded into a bloody, bedraggled ball of feathers and raw meat.

"Don't shoot! Don't shoot!" screamed Zayoud, waving his arms at his men, pirouetting to ensure every soldier had heard his orders. "You might hit the horse!"

Kevin's mouth dropped open—gaping in surprise. And Bolan knew the youth felt betrayed.

He stood there, still shaken to the core, when Bolan seized the reins from his hand and vaulted onto the stallion's back.

Bolan reached down, grabbed Kevin by his shirt and hauled the youngster up in front of him. He would gladly have shot Zayoud then and there, but the sheikh was still restraining his men from killing them. Zayoud himself would buy them the next few seconds they needed....

He nudged the horse, giving the sturdy Malik his head to race for the gateway.

"Stop them!" sputtered Zayoud in frustrated rage. "But no harm must come to my horse!"

The guards at the gateway did not know what they could do, but they were sure their lives would be forfeited if the stallion was injured.

Again, Bolan fired the Uzi from his hip. The man struggling to close the huge wooden doorway collapsed with a bullet in his chest. Another sentry stepped forward, waving in a wild attempt to turn the stallion. Bolan, keeping a tight hold on Kevin, simply rode the man down, sending him spinning in the dust.

Malik's hooves clattered on the cobblestones under the archway. The courtyard erupted into a frenzy behind them.

"Chase them!" yelled the rebel sheikh. The mercs, thinking faster than Zayoud's men, raced for the vehicles.

Bolan checked the great horse lightly, but the sure-footed stallion took the tight L-turn in stride. Kevin patted his neck, urging him faster down the sloping track.

The sentries in the tower above the camp decided to risk firing into the ground ahead of the galloping Malik in an attempt to scare the beast into throwing his riders.

They got off one ragged volley before the bomb beneath the stairs exploded. The upper chamber blew apart. Chunks of granite were hurled through the roof. A cloud of smoke and dust shot into the air. And the topmost floor collapsed into the gaping hole where the steps had been—men, guns, splintered woodwork and shattered stones all went rattling down into the ruined tower.

Bolan was still uncertain whether Kevin was with him now by choice or simply because the abruptly shifting circumstances had left him no option. Kevin was probably too confused to know his own mind. All that mattered was that at this moment he had a tight hold on the youngster as they charged down the track.

The booming explosion within the tower was still ringing in their ears. Bits and pieces of brickwork rained down onto the trail behind them. The falling debris included the rag-doll body of one of the sentries.

Billy Joe Hooker, mad at having accepted the so-called Scarr at face value, was racing forward in the lead Jeep. When the lookout's body flopped on the roadway, the merc bumped right over top of it.

Bolan twisted to snatch a quick look back. They were being chased by slightly more overwhelming odds than he'd counted on—every truck, Jeep and even the armored cars were roaring through the main gates. Stinging clouds of grit and gravel were thrown in the air by the wild group in pursuit of the magnificent steed.

A bullet zipped narrowly past Bolan's head. Malik was only so much horse meat to the angry mercs. They had no real idea of the prestigious bond between Sheikh Zayoud and his most highly prized stallion. They couldn't have cared less; they were in a mood to kill!

The fleeing twosome had a fair lead, but this would evaporate when they stopped to transfer to the Hog. Ruark's gang would be on top of them in no time.

The horse thundered down onto the flat. It was all they could do to hang on. Bolan raced for the dip between the nearest dunes ahead. The strangely eroded rocks were less than six hundred yards beyond.

"Hold tight, Chip!" encouraged Bolan as another string of bullets spouted in the dirt.

Bull Keegan had got their range. The second burst would have struck home if the Arab next to him had not knocked the muzzle skyward, pleading for the stallion's safety. Keegan cuffed the man aside, cursing at his interference, and called for the driver to speed up.

The chase vehicles had cleared the constricting ramp. The leaders were fanning out in line abreast, the drivers jockeying to see who would be first to catch up with the runaways.

The Jeep at the far left suddenly vanished in a shattering fireball, spitting out blazing tracers of burning wreckage. Three mercenaries were dead before their bodies hit the ground. An Arab was thrown clear from the back, stumbled upright on the sand and was mowed down by the truck behind.

Bolan and the boy were both spotted with flecks of sweat from the straining horse.

"Run, Malik, run!" The racing stallion found an extra ounce of effort. Kevin had become a better friend to the courageous animal than Zayoud could ever have guessed.

The skyline ahead of them unexpectedly changed configuration. The immediate horizon seemed to heave upward in the center as the ugly shadow of the Hog appeared menacingly, slewing broadside to a halt on top of the ridge.

Danica Jones leaped back from the driver's seat, waving at Bolan to ride clear of her line of fire. The M-60 opened up with a murderous clatter, spewing out an arc of death in small doses across the sands.

Bolan smiled, elated by her initiative. He had turned Malik to the left and was running flat out into a trough behind the nearest transverse dunes.

Danny's opening salvo caught Hooker's Jeep in the engine. The vehicle rocketed up the shoulder of a dune, seeming to suspend momentarily in midair before it slewed into the path of an oncoming Saracen. The armored car was knocked sideways by the blast of the disintegrating wreck.

The last few seconds ticked away on the preset timers in the ammo shed. The troopers remaining in the yard were caught unaware when the storage dump exploded with crushing force. Mines, grenades, mortars and ammunition touched off one another in an almost instantaneous chain reaction. The whole wall behind the shack cracked from top to bottom.

The sentries, who thought themselves lucky to have a grandstand view of the wild chase, were tossed aside like broken toys by the concussive shock wave. The booming, grinding, shrieking thunderclap was deafening. In that last millisecond more than one man thought it was the end of the world.

Zayoud's driver skidded to a halt below the approach ramp. The sheikh stared in a daze at the dirty mushroom cloud roiling upward, a death's head shadow rearing over the tumbling battlements.

The mercs were not sure what was happening. The castle was exploding behind them. A wildcat had pinned them down with machine-gun fire. And the horse had bolted.

Danny fired another long burst to keep their heads down, jumped back behind the wheel and stamped on the accelerator. She wheeled around off the ridge and chased after Bolan.

They were crossing a hard pan of barren rock. Bolan glanced back and saw the Hog gaining on the outside. He made no move to check the reins as Danny drew alongside.

"You're going to have to jump, Chip!" The youngster stretched out his arm, instinctively grabbing for the corner of the roll bar, and then—before he could think twice—Bolan heaved him aboard the Hog.

Keegan had collected his wits a lot quicker than his colleagues. "Don't let that bastard escape!"

Billy Joe Hooker, bruised and battered by his forcible ejection from the Jeep, limped over to Ruark's vehicle and jumped aboard as the driver took off.

Zayoud was shouting for his own men to follow their lead.

Danny had snatched hold of Kevin's belt to steady the boy as he completed the precarious leap from the galloping horse to the speeding Jeep. She got both hands back on the wheel a fraction before they hit the first bumps of rutted sand.

Bolan leaned sideways and threw himself onto the rear deck of the bouncing Hog.

The Arabian stallion, feeling himself suddenly lightened, slowed to a canter, veered off to the left, heaving for breath after the exhausting run. Kevin glanced back to make sure the riderless horse was all right.

One of the Arab drivers turned off to round up his master's horse. Keegan was screaming in rage at being sidetracked. The other mercs paid it no mind, they pressed on after the smoking dust trail that marked the getaway vehicle.

There was nothing Kevin could do about escaping; he could not jump out at this speed. But Bolan had no way of knowing which side the boy was on now. Before Kevin could protest, Bolan had slipped the cuffs over his wrist and snapped them shut around the roll bar.

The Hog was in good hands. Bolan left the driving to Danny, swung the M-60 around and fired a devastating burst into the convoy chasing after them.

A Jeep swerved in from behind the razor-edged ridge on their flank, bearing down on them fast. Bolan grabbed a grenade and lobbed it in the path of the pursuers. The blast lifted the Jeep onto two wheels and the driver lost control.

A truck loaded with jeering Arabs was gaining ground behind. The driver saw the Jeep start to tilt over crazily in his path. He managed to swerve as the crippled Jeep plowed along on its side, but in avoiding this danger he ran straight over a rock with such a loud crack that even Bolan could hear the impact above the sounds of the furious chase.

The wheels spun on independently, wobbling as they parted ways with the shattered axle. The front end dropped and bulldozed its way deeper into the sand, which curled outward in a cresting bow wave. Scratch one truck.

The men spilled out, but Bolan did not fire into the tumbling mass of Zayoud's troopers. They were being

left well behind now as Danny flew over the knife-
edged summit of a crescent dune.

The Executioner was pleased with Chandler's de-
sign, which was proving its worth. The Hog's four-
wheel drive was most effective across this uneven terrain, the suspension holding firm over the roughest
going.

"You're doing fine, Danny!" Bolan called out from
the rear.

"Anyone on our tail?"

"Uh-uh. You're leaving them standing."

One of the armored cars got off a shot that went
wide. A huge spout of sand erupted to their right.
Danny drove even faster, barreling the sturdy ATV
down the tire tracks that they had followed in at such
a snail's pace.

Bolan remained stationed at the mounted machine
gun. He lost sight of Zayoud's dark Rover. And soon
even Ruark got left behind.

The reddish-gold mounds of the great dunes parted,
revealing a long bare stretch that the winds had flayed
to the skeletal rock. The heat was sweltering. Danny
glimpsed the faint yellow scar of the trail that climbed
the humpback of the jebel ahead of them. She raced
on toward the distant target.

"Take the gully to the left," said Bolan, tapping her
shoulder. There was still no sign of the opposition
when they reached the far end of the barren pan.
"Once we're behind the cover of those next dunes, you
can slow down, then I'll take the wheel."

First he unlocked the steel bracelet that kept Kevin manacled to the roll bar. Bolan decided that it was not safe to keep the youth tied to the Hog.

Kevin massaged his wrist. He had not complained when Bolan first snapped the cuffs on; he did not thank him now for being released. He stared off into the wasteland, still shocked by what had happened, still wondering what was to become of him.

Bolan and Danica Jones accomplished the switch within seconds and were on their way again. All three of them could breathe a little easier now.

"There's a water flask under that seat," Bolan told the boy. "Take a swig and pass it around. I guess it's time we introduced ourselves...."

Bolan and Danny briefly explained who they were and assured Kevin that his safety and well-being were their chief concern. They did not lay a guilt trip on the youngster or even go so far as to paint a detailed portrait of Hassan Zayoud in the colors he deserved; just putting him in the picture and winning his confidence was their first goal. The conversation petered out as both of them could sense Kevin's resentment and resistance.

There was still a long dangerous trek ahead of them, but they had won the first round.

"We're making better time on the way back," joked Danny, trying to lighten the air.

It was true. It had taken nearly four hours of playing cat and mouse with the merc patrols to cover the final leg to Hagadan. Less than forty minutes had elapsed since they had escaped from the fortress and they had already reached the rust-streaked rock that Bolan had noted as a crucial marker.

Bolan wondered if the force of the exploding ammo dump had wrecked the radio tower—if not, then Zayoud could still prepare a warm welcome for the interlopers on the far side of the Jebel Kharg. Or would the sheikh throw all his efforts into the carefully planned coup and risk letting Kevin's rescue crew slip through his fingers? The warrior doubted that Zayoud would be so charitable.

Kevin watched the sloping mass of the barricade rearing up in front of them.

"Where are you taking me?" he asked.

"Just trying to get us all out of Khurabi in one piece."

Bolan became aware of a movement somewhere in that lifeless landscape. He had not been directly focused on it, but he spotted the warning sign. He was sure it was not an animal, not a bird...but a man waiting behind the ridge about five hundred yards ahead. It was the last of the transverse dunes before they reached the foothills trail.

"Danny, take the M-60. Both of you, hang on tight!"

17

The last low trough was coming up on their left.

Bolan tapped on the brakes. They all braced themselves against the retrothrust of their suddenly reduced speed, as the Hog lurched sideways in a power slide.

It would have been a risky maneuver in a two-wheel-drive dune buggy; with a four-wheel system it was dicing with death. But that was better odds than he would get by staying on the track.

They were enveloped in a dark blanket of dust. Bolan had downshifted, keeping up the compression. The Jeep had already straightened out on its new course, charging parallel to the sandbank. Bolan let the revs build tight before he smoothly slotted back into fourth.

The dune looked firm enough. They curved up it and shot the lip head-on.

Bolan trod on the gas until the rear wheels had cleared the pleated summit—this was to stop the Hog nosediving into an end-over-end roll—then he eased off the pedal the second they were airborne, so the revs would not build too high. He kept the wheels straight as they soared more than thirty feet down the lee side.

The Hog landed perfectly and Bolan accelerated, the tachometer swinging wildly toward the red line.

Danny's heart was still stuck in her throat, but she managed to shout, "Over there . . . ambush!"

Craig Harrison and the patrol trucks that had left Hagadan earlier that morning were concealed on either side of the track they would have been on, if it weren't for Bolan's last-minute maneuver.

The desperate detour had swept them safely around the flank of Harrison's death trap. The lookout, who had been fooled by Bolan's off-road expertise, was slip-sliding in giant bounds down the slope to jump aboard the merc's Jeep.

Danny triggered the M-60 and hit the rear truck, which wandered around in a half circle before blowing up.

The Hog crunched up the trail. Bolan was moving too fast over the bumpy track for Zayoud's scouts to get a bead on them. The other truck tried to keep up with Harrison but it was slowly being left behind. Danny decided not to waste any more ammo; she had her hands full hanging on to the roll bar as Bolan climbed the hill with all the speed he could muster.

She kept her eye on the pursuit vehicles as the Hog reached the top of the ravine and began weaving through the scattered boulders. From this higher elevation Danny had a clear view back over the desert floor—not all of the sheikh's forces had given up the chase.

The remaining trucks and Jeeps were spread out now, but the leaders had already reached that last dip where Harrison had planned his ambush.

"Heads down!" Bolan shouted over the noise of the Hog's screaming engine. Random shots were chipping at the rocks as they passed. Harrison was pressing hard on their tail.

Kevin Baker glanced with admiration at the big man driving the ATV. The youth was torn between the excitement of the chase and the pulse-racing fear of real-life danger. It seemed as if at any moment something might go terribly wrong, yet his courage was bolstered by the cool way Bolan reacted to each new threat.

Danny said nothing as they shot diagonally up the last slope leading to the very top of the Jebel Kharg, but she still wondered what on earth Bolan had in mind. To her, it looked as if they were on a one-way street to disaster...they would have to slow down once they topped the crest. Even if Bolan did remember the way through that mined gap, they surely couldn't negotiate it safely at this speed.

They flashed past the small depression from which Bolan and Danny had first surveyed the Forbidden Zone. She did not get a last look back at it; bullets were zinging overhead as they dropped over the skyline.

"Okay, time to hang tough again!" said Bolan, every fiber concentrating on what he had to do in the next few seconds.

The walls of the wind-worn funnel were closing in. Speed mounted as the drop became steeper. Bolan steered right, heading straight for the back of the flat-topped rock that jutted out below them.

There was a slight bump as they dropped off to the boulder—then utter smoothness as they took off from this improvised sandstone ramp.

Bolan had the courage of his convictions. His calculations were correct. They flew over the strip he had forced the brigand to re-mine and hit the sand forty-five feet farther down.

He slowed dramatically, still tracking the Hog straight and true, right into the narrow exit at the bottom of the concealed pass.

Harrison had entered the notch and was coming down the hill full tilt. He followed the natural sweep of the ancient track, swinging wide of the big rock.

The Hog was almost down to a crawl to squeeze through the sharp turn in the cleft when Harrison's Jeep plowed into the realigned mines. The first explosion flung the vehicle against the cliff, then it bounced back and triggered two more of the hidden devices.

The noise of the explosions reverberated between the walls of the cut...and the roaring vibrations brought down huge slabs of the weathered rock.

The truck driver tried to brake as he saw the Jeep first tossed aside by the explosions and then crushed under the collapsing cliff. But he was too late. The heavy truck kept sliding forward, until it was flattened into another piece of debris blocking the passageway.

Bolan was already into the clear on the other side. They saw a dust cloud and lots of loose stones come bounding out of the notch. And a screeching rumble as thousands of tons of rock smothered the trail behind them.

No one would be following them by this route over the Jebel Kharg.

They sped past the campsite hidden behind the swayback ridge, slithering across the loose scree on their downhill run.

Bolan had to fight to keep the Hog from sliding off the trail in places. Three-quarters of the way down the treacherous jebel, he found a shelf that was level enough to halt the vehicle.

"Time to refuel...this is a five-minute pit stop, then we're on our way again."

The dust had billowed up on the crosscurrents of the wind and was now a grayish-yellow smudge smeared across the sky behind them.

"There must be other passes through those hills, someplace farther along," said Bolan. The landslide had only bought them time. They all knew that.

Bolan flattened the last of the empty gas containers and stuffed them into a crevice. He wanted the ATV to be as light as possible for this last lap to the coast.

They shared a little more of the water. Something caught Bolan's attention far off on their left flank. He swept the area through the binoculars. Kevin shaded his eyes and stared in the opposite direction.

"Look, what's that over there?" The youngster pointed toward the disputed frontier.

Bolan swung around. "Camels. Six riders. And they're moving fast."

"Another band of nomads?" asked Danny. Bolan had given the glasses to Kevin.

"I don't think so," said Bolan, "they look more like a long-range border patrol."

"I've seen men like that at the fortress," Kevin told them. "They had a long discussion with Hassan...about four days ago."

"Yeah, and I saw a Khurabi Desert Police plane off that way, flying parallel to the road." Bolan pointed back to the left. "I think the desert police are in this together with Hassan. That plane's probably on the way to pick him up now."

"But how could...?" Danny began.

"It's light enough to use the road as a makeshift landing strip. Zayoud can be back in the city in time to lead his coup."

"And still cut us off before we can escape," added Danny. "But how does that mounted patrol know what's going on?"

"Just because they still ride camels doesn't mean they're not in radio contact. I'm sure they've received orders to intercept us." Bolan glanced at his watch. It was past noon. The race to the coast would be rough going. He walked around the Hog, inspecting it closely for wear and tear. "Okay, all aboard. Kevin, you better take a good look at this Uzi—you may have to use it before this thing is over."

He gave the young man a quick course on the use of the submachine gun as they ran down the final incline and onto the plain. Danny stood in back, keeping watch for any sign of the police patrol. They had gone to earth in the scorching wilderness of shifting sands, mineral beds and broken rocks.

"It hardly looks like it's worth fighting over," remarked Kevin.

"They'll fight and kill for what's underneath it," said Bolan. "And even if the oil wasn't there, they'd still murder one another in the name of blind faith—that and a lust for power. My guess is that the revolt's under way. I wonder how many of the armed forces and the police are going to be fighting on Hassan's side."

"A lot of the more traditionally minded ones probably think his brother has gone soft," said Danny. "Too soft for their liking. Too westernized."

"I don't know what Hassan told you, Chip, or what he pretended to be, but he's not the legitimate ruler of Khurabi. At least, not yet," said Bolan. "The first step is an armed coup to topple the rightful ruler, his elder brother, Sheikh Harun Zayoud. But he's got even bigger plans...and that's where you were to come in. Hassan's already got hold of all the bits and pieces he needs to build a nuclear bomb—you were to provide the know-how. Did he talk to you about that?"

"Yes...yes, he did. Well, a little bit," admitted Kevin. "Nothing specific. You've got to believe me, I didn't know anything about all this."

Kevin chewed on a fingernail, wondering how he could have been so blind. Only now could he analyze step-by-step what had happened to him: the sheer relief at being rescued from the court hearing, the sheikh's generosity and friendly assurances, the adventure of living in a desert castle, the promise of unlimited equipment and all the time he wanted to play with it.

But he had never really wanted to count what all this might cost. Even now Bolan's suggestion seemed too farfetched, almost too fantastic for him to comprehend. Why were grown-ups so dishonest? Is that what Hassan had wanted all the time? Did the sheikh really expect him to build a bomb? Would he have done?

Kevin had no illusions what would have happened to him if he had refused to cooperate. He had seen Hassan's terrible temper in the way he'd treated some of the men. And since that scene this morning in the yard, Kevin knew he didn't really mean that much to Hassan—not as much as a horse, at any rate.

And what of this Mack Bolan guy? Kevin kind of liked Danica, though. But could he trust either of them? He had seen the locket all right, but that could have been stolen, so how did he know they weren't snatching him for their own ends?

Kevin felt very confused.

Alone.

And afraid.

The wind was whipping up the loose sand into a choking fog as they cruised across one of the few level patches. A line of low hillocks seemed to bar the way in front of them.

Danny glanced back through the swirling dust, wondering if all the mercs were now heading for the showdown in Khurabi or if a few of them were still tracking after the Hog. If Hassan Zayoud had not recalled his dogs of war, would Bolan and his group be able to outrun their trackers?

The Hog bounced over a deep rut. Danny swayed to keep her balance. It also saved her life....

A bullet clanged off the roll bar, gouging the metal as it ricocheted past her shoulder.

Bolan accelerated toward a heap of boulders at the base of the nearest rise. The next shot creased his upper arm; a dark stain began to spread along the torn cloth.

He skidded sideways up to the rocks. Kevin jumped out and ducked into the gap between the body of the Hog and the boulder. Danny vaulted over the back and squeezed in with him.

Bolan risked uprooting the M-60 and taking it down from the back. More shots sprayed dirt around the Jeep.

"Here!" Bolan balanced the gun on a smaller stone in front of Danny.

The patrol held the high ground and were in a good position to keep the intruders pinned down until they had a chance to pick them off. Bolan bobbed up once more to grab a couple of items from between the front seats, and this drew more fire from the ridge above.

The noise of the wind was increasing.

"I don't think you'll be able to control the gun without a mount," Bolan told Danny, "but I'm not expecting you to hit anything. Just aim it that way and fire a short burst every ten seconds or so."

"I can keep their heads down," she said.

"You keep your heads down!" Bolan ordered them.

He put on the goggles he had retrieved from the Hog, then began to wind the burnoose around to completely cover his face.

"There's a dust devil building up." His voice was muffled. "And it's going to hit us at any moment. It's the only chance we've got."

"You can't go out there!" protested Danny.

But Bolan was gone. Danny fired two short bursts to provide some initial cover for Bolan.

The heavier particles had formed a low-lying fog rippling across the desert; the lighter dust was boiling up in a twisting mist. The sun was reduced to a molten disk obscured by the thick haze.

Burning-hot granules stung Bolan's skin as he worked his way around the side of the hillock. Some of the sand had penetrated inside his face mask. He could feel it crunching in his teeth. The droning sound was rising in pitch.

He caught only a glimpse of the hilltop between the blasts of wind. Loose stones and grit were being whipped up from the ridge like storm-tossed spray from a wave.

Bolan slipped over the shoulder of the hill. There was a little respite here from the weaker gusts, but it still felt as if the hot breath of hell was blowing over him as he clawed his way through the sand-filled gloom.

The revolving currents of broiling air reached a roaring crescendo. Bolan was being pelted with flying gravel, but he paid little attention. He was more concerned with finding the border-patrol detail and taking them out. He had no misgivings about what these desert police would do to the three Americans if they were found.

Bolan did not like the odds, but with the mounting sandstorm he had the element of surprise.

He would strike first.

A lumpy outline just ahead turned out to be two camels crouching, their long necks stretched low on the ground, waiting for the chaotic storm to blow over them. The small bump beyond the animals was the first KDP patrolman. He turned to try to quiet his mount, when he saw the Executioner. His cry dissolved into the shrieking fury of the twister as Bolan's blade found its mark.

The second target was crouching with his back to the wind. The Executioner's knife sank deep.

The fury was abating as the devilish column of dust began to drift away. Bolan had only moments left before his cover was literally blown.

The KDP captain gave away his position by shouting an order to his comrades. He had found shelter in a small dip near the top of the ridge.

Bolan slid in beside him, stabbing hard with the knife. It must have glanced off an ammunition belt or something the man was wearing under the shroud of his cloak. The border cop twisted around, and with a bellow of rage, rushed Bolan.

The big warrior sidestepped and stuck his leg out, tripping his adversary. The man stumbled, impaling himself on Bolan's knife before he had a chance to recover.

The sky was clearing. The twister was moving rapidly northeast. Bolan saw the other three men huddled along the hilltop. He could not hope to reach them unseen.

One of the men glanced over to where the captain had sheltered, awaiting fresh orders, and realized something was terribly wrong.

He was shouting a warning to his less vigilant companions when Bolan tossed the grenade. Two men took the full force of it, their mutilated bodies being flung back across the dirt.

The sixth man miraculously escaped unscathed. He jumped up, cursing the sheikh's enemies and started to charge down the hillside, loosing a mad volley from his rifle.

Danny watched him coming and pulled the trigger. Calmly she kept on firing. The big weapon bucked and shuddered, shredding the lower slope with looping arcs of white-hot death. The last patrolman was halfway down the incline before he was hit once, twice, three times. His knees buckled and he sprawled forward. The dead body skidded headfirst to the bottom.

Bolan waved that he was all right. Then it was still, almost eerily quiet. The sudden storm had moved on. But the soldier knew the danger was not yet past.

18

"How much farther do we have to go?" asked Kevin. His face looked ashen even beneath the pale mask of sandy grime. He had been shaken up by more than the rattling, bumpy ride.

Bolan checked the instruments. "Twelve miles, maybe less."

Each of them was riding alone with his or her own thoughts. That fracas with the police patrol had cost them more valuable time. Bolan was pushing the Hog as fast as he dared, taking his bearings whenever they crossed the higher ground.

They skirted the cracked, crystalline surfaces of the dried-out mineral beds, raced down a wadi, then churned through a patch of looser gravel.

As they climbed out of a dip, Danny looked back over her shoulder—the rugged heights of the Jebel Kharg were now a dark, jagged line on the horizon, obscured by the glare of the afternoon sun. She turned her head slowly, scanning the horizon. "Look at that smoke!"

Even at this distance three distinct columns of oily smoke were belching up from the direction of the airfield. Bolan nodded to indicate he'd spotted it, too, but said nothing. He figured Zayoud's men had obviously struck their blow for the Crescent Revolution, but there was no point in alarming the others with speculations as to its outcome.

Bolan wondered where Grimaldi was at that moment. The rest of the team involved could be counted on to play their parts, right on the button; it was up to him to stick to the schedule. Still, the fighting around the airfield must be fierce.... Bolan pushed the pedal hard and the Hog hammered down the track.

The sand was softer here, pitted with pebbles. Other vehicles had come this way before, leaving twin sets of tire ruts to follow.

Suddenly the left front end of the Hog sagged, and Bolan fought the wheel as he braked. The dust settled around them. "We have a blown tire."

Bolan jumped out onto the track. The rubber was torn open.

"Kevin, grab the jack." Bolan loosened the spare wheel from its mounting. "See if you can find a couple of flat stones, Danny. We'll need to build a firmer base under that jack."

Danny swung down over the back. She was aware that every second they lost jeopardized not only themselves but the guys who were staging the retrieval operation.

She saw some larger stones that had been smoothed into flattened disks, half buried on the far side of a clear patch of sand. They looked suitable and Danny ran over to get them.

Fifteen feet away from the track the earth seemed to give way under her. The ground was dry, but Danny suddenly felt like she was running through molasses.

The sand, powdery fine, was sucking at her feet. She stumbled to a halt, unable to make headway.

"Mack! Help me, I'm…" The thought froze in her throat. She was being inexorably dragged under.

"Don't struggle, Danny! I'll get you out," shouted Bolan. He dropped the wheel wrench; he had only started to loosen the first nut. "Chip, can you drive?"

Kevin was staring wide-eyed at Danny's predicament. The sand had already swallowed her up to the thighs. He jerked his head to show that he could manage the Hog.

"Back it up a little, no farther than that gravel strip!"

Bolan unbuckled his belt and quickly tugged it free of the loops. Kevin started up the Hog behind him. Testing each step, Bolan worked his way to the very edge of the shingle that seemed to mark the shoreline of this desert dust pool.

Despite Bolan's warning, Danny struggled instinctively against the clammy grip of the quicksand. It was no use. There was nothing to give her purchase; and without anything solid to use as a lever she sank deeper…. The river of powdery sand now lapped at her hips.

Bolan threw the belt out to its full length, stretching as far over the danger spot as he could manage.

Danny bent over, her hand quivering with the effort of reaching out to her fullest extent. There was a maddening gap between her shaking fingers and the tip of the leather lifeline.

"It's no good!" gasped Danny. At least eighteen long inches separated her from the end of the belt. The swirling sand was pouring around her waist. "Your head cloth! Try the head cloth!"

Bolan ripped off the red-checkered burnoose, twirling it into a makeshift rope, and chucked it across the surface.

The efforts to reach the belt had cost Danny dearly; the dust trap was pressing in on her, forcing her down. Now she could not quite reach the rolled-up head cloth...maybe eight, not more than ten inches were all that kept her from grabbing hold. It might as well have been a mile.

Kevin rolled forward cautiously. He did not want to knock Bolan into the same awful dilemma; but the big man looked back and waved him on, then flashed his palm to stop the Hog.

Danny suppressed the urge to scream. She could feel the sand pressing in against the bottom of her ribs. She bit her lip, drawing blood, as she watched Bolan loop his belt around the front fender.

He jumped forward; the sand quickly covered his boots but he sank no farther. With the end of the belt twisted around his wrist, Bolan leaned as far as he could across the death trap. He worked his free arm in a semicircle, slapping down the head cloth in a straight line between himself and Danny.

She snatched hold of the end. There was just enough to loop it once around her wrist and hold tight. "Got it!"

Bolan began to exert pressure, doing his best to drag her bodily from the grip of the quicksand. She didn't budge. She had stopped sinking.

Danny felt as if her arm was going to be torn from its socket as Bolan built up the strain.

Bolan grunted, shaking his head to clear the sweat from his eyes as he kept urging Danny on. "Try to wriggle your hips free. Lean down on the surface a little more . . . I've got hold of you!"

He was blind to all else but saving this woman. They had just been across hell and back together—Bolan wasn't going to lose her now.

"It's working!" cried Danny. She knew her life depended on the next few seconds. She buckled over, trying to kick with her legs, as Bolan manhandled her toward the shore. It was almost like swimming, but in painfully slow motion.

Inch by inch Danny was moving closer to his outstretched arm. . . . He let go of the head cloth and clasped her hand.

"One last effort, Danny!"

"Why don't you leave the little lady right there?" The words cut through the air like a knife. Then Ruark chuckled. "After all, it'll save us a bullet."

Ruark, Billy Joe Hooker and two of Zayoud's soldiers stood on the knoll overlooking the deadly quicksand.

Bolan paid no heed to the order. He kept on pulling and knew he was making headway. Danny was definitely coming free. He heard the ominous click as the bodyguards cocked their weapons and brought them to bear.

"You're not going anywhere, fella, so just drop her back in the soup." Ruark did not like to be ignored, especially when he had the whip hand. "Just heard over the radio that your buddy's about to land at the airfield. Zayoud might have gone off at half cock, but there should be a nice welcome waiting for your plane.''

Billy Joe snickered and Bolan knew he was just itching to pull the trigger.

''Hey you, kid,'' snapped Ruark. ''Get out of that Jeep.''

''Stay where you are, Chip. Don't move,'' countermanded Bolan. He could crook his arm now, Danny was almost home free. ''You were in that mess around Khe Phong, weren't you, Ruark?''

''Yeah . . .'' What the hell did this guy know about that?

''And you got a Purple Heart, didn't you?''

''What the hell's that to you? Yeah, I was wounded at Khe Phong.''

''Then this little lady, as you call her, might just be one of the women who patched you up!''

Ruark was stunned; even the muzzle of his gun dropped slightly to one side.

Danny seized hold of Bolan's arm as he dragged her onto the gravel.

Billy Joe Hooker waved his rifle at the Hog. ''Cap'n told you to climb out of there, kid. Do it!''

This time Kevin did as he was told. He stood up, his head hung meekly, ashamed to be giving in to these bullies. No one expected him to be holding the Uzi.

Ruark was still trying to place the big guy with the piercing blue eyes when the first long burst hit him in the chest. He died with a puzzled frown creasing his forehead.

Hooker was nicked in the side. He spun around and dropped his weapon in surprise at the stinging pain.

Kevin's lips were drawn back tightly. He uttered an unintelligible scream and kept on firing. The withering hail of bullets cut down Zayoud's men; one peppered in the abdomen, the other dying with a shot through the face.

The magazine was exhausted.

The boy stood there, gripping the top of the wheel, trying to stop trembling.

Danny sat leaning against the front of the Hog, too drained to move.

Bolan ran up the short slope and picked up the nearest rifle. Billy Joe Hooker was whimpering for mercy. He was on his knees, rocking back and forth, holding a blood-smeared hand against his side.

"On your feet, Hooker! You've got a tire to change."

19

Billy Joe Hooker was forced to drag the bodies of his comrades out of sight behind the knoll. Bolan threw their weapons into the sinkhole and watched them disappear under the hungry sands while the Southerner, still pleading for his life, changed the ruined tire.

Danny went to make sure Kevin was all right. The youngster had walked on farther down the track. His eyes were watery and he still shook with spasms of dry-retching at the thought of what he had done.

Before today death had been something he had only seen on TV: playacting on the detective shows, or sometimes for real on the news. It was difficult to tell the difference. The toll in nuclear war was measured in megadeaths—figures so large they were meaningless. But until now Death had never touched him, involved him, used him as its agent....

Kevin had never liked Ruark much, as the man strutted around the castle, but he would never forget that look on Ruark's face or the way he poked an accusing finger at Kevin as he collapsed on the slope back there.

"You did what had to be done, Kev," Danny said to him. "You saved our lives. It was very brave of you to stand up to them."

Kevin did not feel at all heroic. He still felt sick to his stomach.

"Are you brave enough to stand up for yourself? I'm sure things can be worked out. I'll be there and I'm going to speak up for you."

Kevin nodded. He did not turn to face her. He had to blink quickly to stop the tears threatening to trickle out. She was touching his arm; he placed his hand on top of hers—yes, he wanted to go home.

"Ready to roll!" Bolan called out.

They trotted back to the Jeep together and climbed aboard.

"Hey, what about me?" whined Billy Joe.

"You're not worth a bullet. You can walk," said Bolan. He prodded the wounded merc, pointing to the quicksand patch.

Danny knew all too vividly the living horror of those sinking sands. "Please, Mack, no...."

Hooker stood there sweating it out.

The chilling gaze of those ice-blue eyes never wavered, but Bolan relented. He tossed his head and growled, "Back off—you're on your own."

Bolan stomped on the gas. The back wheels spewed a ton of grit all over the stranded Hooker.

JACK GRIMALDI WAS STILL far out over the sea when he spotted the black smoke smudge. It did not stop him from proceeding with the final approach. Everything had to be by the book. He tried raising the tower—but only got some garbled Arabic and an earful of static.

As he lost altitude over the gulf shallows he could pick out a ragged convoy beating a hasty retreat toward the airfield. There was more fighting along the coast road.

Grimaldi knew he was only a diversion, a means of distracting Hassan's attention, but right now it looked as if the rebel forces were already on the run. Of course, he would not put it past Bolan to have routed all of them single-handed.

Wheels down. Grimaldi adjusted the flaps. He was perfectly positioned above the runway.

Jack was already pulling back on the controls. It did not look as if Mack needed him to stage a fake landing; these dogs were running off with their tails between their legs.

Grimaldi lifted off.

BOLAN AND HIS TWO COMPANIONS could see the low, square outline of Abdel's house and the electrified compound fence beyond it. The dog came running across the scrub, yapping madly and chasing after them as Bolan drove around the corner to the gate.

The company watchman waved at Danica and hurried over with the key. Hamad, his brother, stood in the doorway, barring it with his arm to prevent the women and children from leaving the safety of the house. The little girl clutched at her uncle's trouser leg, peering around to watch what was happening.

"You're back! You'll be safe here, Professor Jones," promised Abdel, who apparently thought they had come to claim sanctuary in the Allied Oil storage depot.

"What's happening?" asked Danny. "Have you any news?"

"Terrible trouble," said Abdel, casting an apologetic look toward the heavens, "even if it is the will of Allah. There's been an uprising in the city. Hamad was driving the truck in . . . he had to turn back. The radio station has changed hands three times already."

"Has anybody been up here yet?" Bolan demanded as he strode over toward the top of the gravel track.

"No, *sah'b*. Some soldiers went past below." Abdel grinned. "I cheered for Zayoud . . . one of them must win."

Bolan examined the coast road through his glasses. The dark blob of a fast-moving car snapped into focus. It was another Rover—dark blue this time— fleeing the city and heading straight for them.

Since they had not showed at the airport, it should not have been too difficult to figure out their likely whereabouts. Bolan was not going to hang around to find out if Hassan wanted to settle a personal score with him, or if he wanted to use the boy as a hostage. He probably had both in mind.

"Abdel, get your family under cover. Don't show yourselves. Don't leave them, understand?"

"Yes, *sah'b*, but . . ."

"Just do it."

Bolan ran back to the Hog. The guard had left the gates open for him. He drove into the compound, swung past the stacked pipes and crates and drew up outside the shed.

"Help me with that other door."

Danny and Kevin tugged open the door on their side as Bolan pulled back the right-hand door. The air inside was stifling.

Danny gasped—it looked almost comical. Sitting in the center of the floor was the ultralight aircraft Bolan had assembled from Red Chandler's kit. The tubes and fabric he had claimed were tents made up the wings and open frame of the specially designed plane; the so-called generator was its power plant.

Bolan tested the controls. He flipped the switches exactly as memorized.

"Hop in, Kevin." There were only two canvas bucket seats. "You're going to have to sit on Danny's lap."

"Can this carry all three of us?"

"That's what we're about to find out."

The plane started forward with a jerk, then began to roll more smoothly down the incline. Bolan risked one quick look back through the dust cloud they were blowing out across the yard. The Rover came swinging through the gates. Its body was streaked with grime and pockmarked with half a dozen bullet holes. The driver aimed to smash them sideways.

Bolan coaxed the last reserve of power from the little engine.

Danny shut her eyes. They were twenty feet from the sheer drop at the end of the bluff.

Zayoud leaned out the window, firing a pistol wildly at the spindly aircraft. A couple of slugs flew through the skeleton framework.

Bolan eased back on the stick. The ultralight ran off the edge, lurched downward for a sickening second and then, borne on an updraft, it leveled out....

The sheikh was shouting for his chauffeur to turn away, but his warning came too late. The crumbling cliff edge collapsed and the heavy car plunged down.

Mack Bolan and the others were clear of the coastal road when Hassan's car struck the concrete and exploded.

The trio in the small aircraft were already out over the sea. Fishermen looked up from the deck of their *dhow*, and Bolan could see the amazed expressions on their faces as the strange flying machine skimmed over their mast.

"We're losing height, Mack," said Danny, then wished she hadn't—the comment was superfluous.

"We're not going to get too far in this contraption," added Kevin. He did not care who knew it: he was scared.

They were about a mile from shore and barely thirty feet above the waves.

"You can swim, can't you, Chip?"

"No, I never learned how."

It had not occurred to Bolan that a boy living in Florida might not have learned to take care of himself in the ocean. "Well, you can just tread water. Hang on to me, it won't be long...."

Danny glanced in the direction Bolan had indicated. A big, beautiful seaplane—with Steve Hohenadel and his partner at the controls—was coming to pick them up.

She was still watching it when Bolan pancaked the ultralight into the warm water of the gulf.

20

Danny was in her office at Westfield, staring at the photograph of the crusader fortress on the rock at Hagadan, when the phone rang.

It was Salim Zakir.

"You left without saying farewell, Danica," he chided her.

She didn't know what to say. "I, er—well, I..."

Zakir interrupted with a hearty chuckle. "The videotape you gave me to hand over to the sheikh was all the evidence Harun needed to confirm our suspicions about his brother. We knew he was plotting something and—thanks to you and, er, your colleague—we were ready to deal with the emergency."

Danny had already seen the story in the newspaper. It did not even rate the front page. The report was buried in the back of the international news section.

"Allied Oil are being given full credit for their assistance in this affair," Zakir told her. "Mr. Patterson is flying over to receive a decoration to show our gratitude."

Danny could imagine that the oil executive would be happily bragging about this at parties for years to come.

"We've also retrieved your Jeep—it's quite an amazing vehicle—and this will, of course, be returned to you in America. Sheikh Harun Zayoud does wonder if he might acquire such a Jeep for himself."

"I'll see what I can do...I shall have to speak to Professor Bolan."

"And when will you be coming to visit us again, Danica?"

"Oh, I'm not sure...one day."

As soon as Zakir hung up, Danny dialed the number Bolan had given her.

It rang and rang.

No answer.

And although she was disappointed, somehow, she was not surprised.

MORE ADVENTURE NEXT MONTH WITH

MACK BOLAN

#88 Baltimore Trackdown

Law reform—Bolan style

A police chief betrays his code of honor to the Mafia and tries to persuade fellow officers to accept money from the Mob. Those who refuse are killed.

Through all his miles along the hellfire trail, the Executioner has always looked on the police as soldiers of the same side.

But Mack Bolan sees this lawman as a traitor, both to his badge and to Bolan's cause. Will the warrior break his own rules to stop the corrupt cop?